Completeness

Itamar Moses

A SAMUEL FRENCH ACTING EDITION

SAMUEL FRENCH
FOUNDED 1830

SAMUELFRENCH.COM
SAMUELFRENCH-LONDON.CO.UK

FOR PRODUCTION ENQUIRIES

UNITED STATES AND CANADA
Info@SamuelFrench.com
1-866-598-8449

UNITED KINGDOM AND EUROPE
Theatre@SamuelFrench-London.co.uk
020-7255-4302

Each title is subject to availability from Samuel French, depending upon country of performance. Please be aware that COMPLETENESS may not be licensed by Samuel French in your territory. Professional and amateur producers should contact the nearest Samuel French office or licensing partner to verify availability.

MUSIC USE NOTE

IMPORTANT BILLING AND CREDIT REQUIREMENTS

COMPLETENESS had its New York City premeire produced Off Broadway by Playwrights Horizons on September 13th, 2011 with Artistic Director, Tim Sanford and Managing Director Leslie Marcus. The performance was directed by Pam MacKinnon, with scenic and costume designs by David Zinn, lighting by Russell Champa, and sound by Bray Poor. The Production Stage Manager was Charles M Turner III. The cast was as follows:

ELLIOT . . . . Karl Miller
MOLLY . . . . Aubrey Dollar
LAUREN/KATIE/NELL. . . . . Meredith Forlenza
DON/CLARK/FRANKLIN. . . . . Brian Avers

COMPLETENESS was originally produced by South Coast Repertory in Costa Meza, CA on April 17th, 2011 with Artistic Director, Marc Masterson; Founding Directors, David Emmes and Martin Benson; and Managing Director, Paula Tomei. The production was directed by Pam Mackinnon, with set design by Christopher Barreca, lighting by Russell. H. Champa, and sound by Bray Poor. The Production Stage Manager was Jennifer Ellen Butler. The cast was as follows:

ELLIOT . . . . Karl Miller
MOLLY . . . . Mandy Siegfried
LAUREN/KATIE/NELL. . . . . .Brooke Bloom
DON/CLARK/FRANKLIN. . . . . Johnathan McClain

Originally commissioned by the Manhattan Theatre Club, Lynne Meadow, Artistic Director; Barry Grove, Executive Producer; Paige Evans, Director of New Play Development, with funds provided by the Alfred P. Sloan Foundation.

CHARACTERS

ELLIOT

MOLLY

LAUREN/KATIE/NELL

DON/CLARK/FRANKLIN

A NOTE ABOUT PROJECTIONS

The script calls for projections at one key moment in scene eight. If your production is using projections, however, it's not necessary to limit their use to that one moment, they can be used in various creative ways in transitions throughout the show, or even during the entrance of Clark and Katie in scene seven, to help bring out some of the metaphorical resonances of the science discussed in the script. On the other hand, if your production is unable to use projections for whatever reason, this doesn't mean you can't produce the play: other elements, lights, set, and especially sound (perhaps the text to be projected is instead recorded in the voices of the actors?) can also be used.

A NOTE ABOUT THE BREAKDOWN

The simulated "breakdown" of the play at the end of scene eight is something every production is going to have to solve in its own way, and any specific stage directions there in the script are just a basic guideline. It seems desirable, however, to genuinely trick the audience at first, and then somehow, by the end of the "improvisatory" dialogue that follows, to bring about a dawning (or even sudden) awareness that this, too, might be scripted. In any case, be prepared for a lot of people to tell you that this is their least favorite part of the play and that the play would be better without it. This is how you will know you did it right.

1.

(the public computer cluster)

(Rows of tables with computers, or at least the suggestion of this. Ugly fluorescent lighting. ELLIOT sits at a computer, working. He types for a while. Then clicks the mouse button to run something – a program of some kind? Then stares at the screen and waits.)

(He waits for a while. He shifts, annoyed. He clicks the mouse again. Then a few more times. Is the thing frozen? Frustrated, ELLIOT sighs. And restarts the computer. He gets up. He puts on his jacket, which is hanging on the back of the chair, picks up his backpack from where it is on the floor, and has just turned to go when...)

(...MOLLY enters and sits down at a different computer, nearby. ELLIOT hesitates. Then he pretends he has just arrived: puts his backpack down on the floor, puts his jacket over the back of the chair, sits at the computer, and pretends to start doing something, too.)

(ELLIOT and MOLLY both work in silence for a while. MOLLY is intent on her screen, reading, and then typing. ELLIOT is less intent on his screen and keeps sneaking glances at MOLLY. Then MOLLY sends an email. Her computer makes a "send" noise.)

ELLIOT. Email.

MOLLY. Excuse me?

ELLIOT. Sending, uhhh...

(Then, ELLIOT just looks down, lapsing back into awkward silence, and pretending to work some more. MOLLY rereads something on her screen and then sits back, annoyed.)

MOLLY. *(quietly)* Not *again.*

ELLIOT. Is there a problem?

MOLLY. What?

ELLIOT. Is there a problem with the computer? Because I'm a C.A. I mean, I'm a grad student? In Computer Science? But I also work as a... So if there's –

MOLLY. There's no problem with the computer.

ELLIOT. Oh okay. *(beat)* I'm Elliot.

MOLLY. What?

ELLIOT. Sorry, just, I totally ambushed you without even... I'm Elliot?

MOLLY. There's not a problem with the computer, Elliot. Thanks.

ELLIOT. Okay.

MOLLY. Okay.

*(A moment. **MOLLY** gets back to work. **ELLIOT**, internally kicking himself, starts to get back to pretend work, but then just shakes his head, gets up, grabs his jacket, and is reaching for his backpack, when:)*

MOLLY. I'm Molly.

ELLIOT. What? Oh –

MOLLY. Sorry, I can be...that was rude. I'm Molly.

ELLIOT. Oh, no. I mean: it's nice to meet you, Molly.

MOLLY. It's nice to meet you too, Elliot.

*(A moment. **MOLLY** offers her hand for a handshake. **ELLIOT** shakes **MOLLY**'s hand.)*

ELLIOT. All right. *(beat)* So, all right, um...

*(A moment. **ELLIOT** walks away. A few moments pass. **MOLLY** types some more. **ELLIOT** comes back.)*

I just...forgot my...

*(**ELLIOT** goes to get his backpack, which he left on the floor by his chair. Then he nods one more time, at nothing in particular, and has turned to go, when:)*

MOLLY. Hey, Elliot, let me ask you something.

ELLIOT. What? Yeah, okay.

MOLLY. Do you know what a two-hybrid screen is?

(beat)

ELLIOT. Um –

MOLLY. Actually it doesn't matter.

ELLIOT. No, it's, you know, some kind of...method... whereby – ?

MOLLY. No that's not actually my question.

ELLIOT. Oh thank god.

MOLLY. Let's say you've accumulated a ton of data from an experiment. But the data is so sort of noisy and full of crap that it is very very difficult to know what it means. Don't you guys have ways of mitigating that?

ELLIOT. What guys? You mean in C.S.?

MOLLY. *(overlapping)* I, computer guys, yeah.

ELLIOT. Um, maybe. What's your project?

MOLLY. I work with yeast cultures, primarily? I –

ELLIOT. *Yeast* cultures? Seriously?

MOLLY. What.

ELLIOT. No, just, okay.

MOLLY. It's how we study protein-protein interactions. Which are responsible for more or less every process in your body.

ELLIOT. *(catching up)* This is Molecular Biology.

MOLLY. Yeah. Yeast is just a hospitable environment in which to perform *screens*. Of proteins we *know* against proteins we *don't*. Bait and prey.

ELLIOT. Huh. I like that, "Bait and pray." Kind of mystical for science, but –

MOLLY. No, *prey*. Like, *prey*. Like –

ELLIOT. *(overlapping)* Oh, oh, *prey*.

MOLLY. *(miming one creature pouncing on another)* Bait and prey.

ELLIOT. Gotcha.

MOLLY. Yeah. You use yeast as your host and plate a bunch of lines of a known protein, that's your bait, and then you *criss*-cross that with *unknown* protein strains, that's your prey, to make a grid. And then you add a reporter gene that causes a phenotype change? *Only where the proteins bind.* So at most of the intersections nothing happens, but... *(She begins rummaging in her bag.)* where two of the little guys *do* interact...when there's a *pathway* there...hold on... Ah.

ELLIOT. Ah!

*(Because **MOLLY** has suddenly pulled a Petri dish out of her bag and, because **ELLIOT** was leaning in, she has held it up a little bit too near his face for comfort.)*

MOLLY. Oh god, sorry!

ELLIOT. Yeah, is that – ?

MOLLY. Yeah, no, don't worry, it's totally sterile, it's just... Here. Look.

*(Tentatively, **ELLIOT** looks.)*

ELLIOT. It's blue.

MOLLY. Well it *turns* blue. Or it does whatever the reporter gene you chose tells it to do. I like blue.

ELLIOT. And then you know which proteins interact.

MOLLY. Well that's the problem because maybe not. My advisor keeps saying –

ELLIOT. Noisy and full of crap.

MOLLY. Exactly.

ELLIOT. Yeah. What you need is a data mining algorithm.

MOLLY. Okay. Say more.

ELLIOT. Where a computer looks at your data and then tells you the most likely interpretation of it.

MOLLY. I *do* need that. *Thank* you. *(writing it down)* "Data... mining...algorithm."

ELLIOT. *(overlapping)* I mean, I'd of course need actually to look at your data to figure out what specific kind you *need*, but, generally speaking –

MOLLY. What?

ELLIOT. Oh, well, just, I'd, um –

MOLLY. I, oh, no, sorry, I didn't, uh… *(beat)* I didn't mean *you.*

ELLIOT. Oh. *(beat)* Yeah, no, just, if –

MOLLY. Yeah I didn't mean you *personally.* Or, I mean, I should probably, like, go through the department, or –

ELLIOT. Oh, no, yeah.

MOLLY. Or through both of our departments in, like, some official *way.*

ELLIOT. Yeah, no, of course.

MOLLY. Yeah so… *(beat)* Why, would you *do* that for me?

ELLIOT. Uh, yeah. I mean, yeah, sure. If you want.

   (beat)

MOLLY. Okay.

ELLIOT. Okay, great, um, how can I get in touch with you?

MOLLY. What?

ELLIOT. What's the best way to get in touch with you?

MOLLY. I'm sitting right here. Like, now, in front of you, so –

ELLIOT. No, I know, I mean, later, to set up, like, a –

MOLLY. Oh, yeah, no, right, of course, here, let me…this is my cell.

   *(**MOLLY** tears off a corner of one page of her notebook and jots down her phone number. She slides it across the table to **ELLIOT**.)*

ELLIOT. Great. *(beat)* Actually could I have your email address?

   *(**ELLIOT** slides the paper back.)*

MOLLY. Oh. Um. Okay.

ELLIOT. Sorry, just, I'm more likely to actually…I'm a little more comfortable –

MOLLY. That's…fine. Here.

(**MOLLY** *writes down her email address and slides the paper back.*)

ELLIOT. Great. Thanks.

(**ELLIOT** *looks at the paper. Then he leans forward and types something into his computer. Then he clicks with the mouse and there is a "send" noise. A moment.* **ELLIOT** *nods and half-smiles awkwardly at* **MOLLY** *who half-smiles back perplexed. Then the email arrives at the computer in front of* **MOLLY** *with an "arrival" noise.*)

MOLLY. Oh!

ELLIOT. Yeah, that's, um. That's me

(*…transition…all the transitions cast the space into a dark blue light…*)

2.

(ELLIOT 's place)

(The whole apartment is really one space: front door, kitchen area, sleeping area, work area with desk and computer. Another door presumably leads to the bathroom. Also, there is a white board on the wall with a to-do list written on it. LAUREN is in bed, in pajamas of some kind, working on her laptop. ELLIOT is at his desk, at the computer, in a t-shirt and boxers maybe, or otherwise dressed for bed. He is on his cell phone.)

ELLIOT. Uh-huh...uh-huh...well yeah I mean, nobody wants to feel that way...

(ELLIOT smiles at LAUREN, rolling his eyes. She smiles, understanding.)

Uh-huh...uh-huh...oh, I'm sure that's not true, I'm sure you both want it to work. I mean, you're not the easiest guy to... No, I know, I just mean she's *been* there, through all your...uh-huh.

(ELLIOT shakes his head at LAUREN apologetically. She shrugs: "No problem.")

Uh-huh.... *(then, a little exasperated)* Well then why don't you guys just get *divorced* then? ...*(relenting)* I, no, I didn't, I'm just...uh-huh...uh-huh, I, oh, uh, Lauren just came over...

(LAUREN smirks and nods: "Great. Use me." ELLIOT shrugs: "Sorry!")

Yeah, so I should...okay...okay...I will...okay...bye.

(ELLIOT hangs up the phone. Then:)

My Dad says hi.

(LAUREN nods. Then:)

LAUREN. Does it ever *bother* your Mom?
ELLIOT. What.
LAUREN. That he has these conversations with you.

ELLIOT. Should it?

LAUREN. It would bother me.

ELLIOT. Huh. *(beat)* Yeah I don't know.

(**ELLIOT** *gets back to work.* **LAUREN** *works. A silence. Then:*)

LAUREN. What are you working on?

ELLIOT. An algorithm.

LAUREN. For the TSP?

ELLIOT. No, not for me, it's a data mining algorithm. For an experiment.

LAUREN. What experiment?

ELLIOT. On yeast?

LAUREN. *Yeast?* Who's working on yeast?

ELLIOT. I know, right? Just some grad student, just this grad student, in bio.

LAUREN. Do I know him?

ELLIOT. Uhh… *(beat)* No, I don't think you do. *(beat)* I mean, it's pretty standard, pretty basic heuristics, so I can just…adapt existing code? But it's a nice change of *pace*, to, you know, work on something *else.*

LAUREN. *And* it might be good, for the department, which *funds* you, to see you branch out a little, yeah. *(pause)* Hey.

ELLIOT. What.

(**LAUREN** *closes her laptop and puts it away.*)

LAUREN. Come here.

(**ELLIOT** *looks over.* **LAUREN** *is looking at him suggestively.*)

ELLIOT. In, yeah, in just a second.

LAUREN. Uhh –

ELLIOT. No, I just, I'm almost…hey, no…

(*Because* **LAUREN**, *feeling rejected, puts her laptop away, flicks off a light, and pretends to go to sleep, while in fact sulking. A moment.*)

ELLIOT. Seriously. Just one second.

(No answer. **ELLIOT** *looks back at the computer. Then back at* **LAUREN**. **ELLIOT** *leaves the computer still working, crosses to the bed, and slips under the covers.)*

ELLIOT. Hey.

LAUREN. *(muffled)* No.

ELLIOT. No? Just no?

LAUREN. No.

ELLIOT. "No" in reference to what, exactly?

LAUREN. No don't come over here.

(A moment. **ELLIOT** *gets out of bed and heads back to the computer.)*

LAUREN. Oh my god! Elliot!

ELLIOT. What? You pushed me away!

LAUREN. *So?*

ELLIOT. So you're mad that I'm not in bed and then you're mad that I am in bed and now you're mad that I got out of bed?

LAUREN. No! I'm mad that you didn't *stay* in bed and try to make me *feel* better!

(A moment. **ELLIOT** *starts to move back towards the bed.)*

LAUREN. Oh my god what's *wrong* with you?

ELLIOT. *What? You just said – !*

LAUREN. Yes so don't come back when I *tell* you to! Come back when you *want* to!

ELLIOT. But..! I...! *(pause)* I do want to.

LAUREN. No you *don't.*

ELLIOT. Okay so let me get this. Now that you've told me to come back to bed, my decision to return is thus rendered, *a priori*, meaningless.

LAUREN. Well –

ELLIOT. Because you do realize that, by *that* logic, once you've expressed a preference, I can never actually *do* what you prefer without my motives being suspect.

LAUREN. Well, okay, but –

ELLIOT. On top of which, the fact that my return to bed was *preceded* by you telling me you *want* me to does not necessarily mean that your *telling* me was the *cause*. Correlation is not causation.

LAUREN. I know that, Elliot. I'm just telling you how it *feels*.

ELLIOT. And, and! In *any* case: what's *wrong* with me just wanting to give you what you *want?* Don't you *want* me to…want to give you what you want?

LAUREN. I…guess, but –

ELLIOT. So okay then.

LAUREN. So, wait, so then which is it?

ELLIOT. Which is what.

LAUREN. Is it that you really want to come to bed or that you're trying to give me what I want by coming to bed?

(beat)

ELLIOT. My point is that either way there's nothing for you to get upset about.

LAUREN. But I *am* upset.

ELLIOT. Okay.

LAUREN. Is the flaw in your theory.

ELLIOT. Well –

LAUREN. Because, you know what? Because it doesn't *feel* like you trying to do *either* of those things. It *feels* like you just trying to *prevent* me from getting *mad*.

ELLIOT. Well maybe that's because you're always on the *brink* of getting mad at me and so sometimes *preventing* that feels like the absolute best that I can do.

LAUREN. But it isn't! You can make me happy!

ELLIOT. *How!?*

LAUREN. I don't want to have to *tell* you!

ELLIOT. Right because you *want* me to just *guess!*

LAUREN. No. I *want* you. To just. *Know.*

(pause)

ELLIOT. Well…

> *(A moment. **ELLIOT** shuts his eyes, rubs his forehead, something like that.)*

LAUREN. What. What is it.

ELLIOT. No, just…I feel a little nauseous.

LAUREN. Elliot. What is it.

> *(A moment. **ELLIOT** is not looking at **LAUREN**. Then his computer starts to make a little noise, a gentle ticking, as though its hard drive is straining a little, or as though its a fan has turned on to cool it. Something like that. For a moment or two, **ELLIOT**, lost in thought, doesn't notice. But then it jars him out of his reverie. He hits whatever buttons are necessary to stop the computer from doing whatever it's doing, and, with that:)*

ELLIOT. All right, look. I've just, um. I've just been… thinking? About what kind of, like, situation, or relationship, you seem to want to be in.

LAUREN. What? What does that mean.

ELLIOT. Well, and, just that, if *I* don't know if that's the same kind of situation that *I* want to be in, necessarily, then it doesn't, like, seem exactly *fair*. To you. To not let you, like, go, and *find* that kind of relationship. Or situation.

LAUREN. Um –

ELLIOT. You know?

LAUREN. Well, not…I mean, look, Elliot, I don't know what you mean exactly, I mean, I don't have some, like, abstract *kind* of relationship that I wish to *be* in, if, you know, if something about the way…I want to, this is, so if, like, if the parameters… If something is making you uncomfortable then we can, you know, I can try to…or, I mean, I'm sorry I, it's not a big deal, we don't have to even…I have this stupid *cold* that's been… don't think you have to like set me *free* to find, like, some guy I haven't even *met* yet who'll, like, I don't even know what. *(beat)* What are you saying?

(beat)

ELLIOT. What I'm *saying* is. I feel like if I don't know if I'm going to be a certain kind of guy for you. Like if I know that I'm *not* going to be that guy. It seems like I should say that. Like. As soon as possible.

LAUREN. *(quietly)* Yeah but what does that mean, though, "be that guy for me."

ELLIOT. Who'll want to turn this into...something permanent. *(beat)* Because, if –

LAUREN. Oh my god, what am I doing in your *bed?*

(**LAUREN** *gets out of bed and moves as far away from* **ELLIOT** *as she can get.*)

ELLIOT. Hey –

LAUREN. Uh, no, I think I've, I think I got it, sorry, it took me –

ELLIOT. *(moving toward her)* No, listen to me.

LAUREN . Oh my god, get away from me.

(**ELLIOT** *stops where he is.*)

LAUREN. What.

(beat)

ELLIOT. You're amazing, okay? I think you're great.

LAUREN. Oh my god – !

ELLIOT. But, okay, but would you please just listen?

LAUREN. I...! Get away from me!

(*Because* **ELLIOT** *is moving towards her again, so she shoves past him, and backs away to the other side of the room.*)

ELLIOT. Okay! Okay. I just, look, I just want to –

LAUREN. No! Don't tell me how great I am, okay? Don't do that.

ELLIOT. Okay.

LAUREN. Okay.

(beat)

ELLIOT. Okay so then –

LAUREN. So wait so are you saying that you're not the kind of guy who will want something to be permanent, like, *ever* with *anyone*, like, that's just not something you're going to want to *do*, or are you saying it's not something you can see yourself doing with *me* because of something that you think isn't *right* for you *about* me.

(beat)

ELLIOT. Well, that's, you know, that's not really a question that's possible to answer, is it.

LAUREN. It's not?

ELLIOT. Well, what, you want me to stand here and tell you that I will never want to stay with anyone, ever, because – ?

LAUREN. No, of course not –

ELLIOT. *(overlapping)* Because I mean, obviously, every relationship I've been in up to now has, you know, *ended*, I mean, mani*fes*tly, so –

LAUREN. *(overlapping)* Right, of course, but –

ELLIOT. But does that mean they *all* will, *always*, how should *I* know?

LAUREN. No, of course not, Elliot, I am not asking you to *predict* the *future!* I'm asking you if...! *(Pause. Maybe she starts to cry.)* What did I do *wrong?*

ELLIOT. You didn't do anything wrong.

LAUREN. No, I must have done something, I must have done something wrong, tell me what I did wrong.

ELLIOT. You didn't do anything wrong, it's, you know... timing.

LAUREN. Timing?

ELLIOT. Yeah.

LAUREN. How is it *timing?*

ELLIOT. Well you knew that I was coming off a really bad break-up.

LAUREN. Right. I mean, so was I.

ELLIOT. And well right but –

LAUREN. I mean, we *talked* about it, we were like, hey, isn't it surprising and unexpected to be able to get into something with someone new, we *talked* about it –

ELLIOT. Yeah, it was, it is.

LAUREN. So, right, so then what the fuck is your point exactly?

ELLIOT. That maybe...

LAUREN. What.

ELLIOT. I mean don't you ever feel...

LAUREN. *What. Tell* me.

ELLIOT. Don't you ever feel like there are certain feelings inside you, that are curled up inside you, like a potential, and can stretch out and attach to another person. And when those feelings get bruised or hurt they curl back up again until they heal. And until that happens they aren't available. But maybe a *different* kind of feeling is, one that isn't bruised, and you attach in that way, but meanwhile, the other part of you, the bruised part, is healing, and then eventually, it's healed. And you feel that potential again.

(*beat*)

LAUREN. Oh my god –

ELLIOT. No, just, because, listen –

LAUREN. I'm, you're saying I'm, get *away* from me –

(**ELLIOT** *reaches for* **LAUREN**'s *hand but she pulls away and heads for the bathroom.*)

ELLIOT. But don't you feel that?

LAUREN. You're saying I'm a *rebound*?

ELLIOT. No, just, first of all, I don't really like that word?

LAUREN. Oh my god!

ELLIOT. I don't, I think that it's reductive!

LAUREN. Oh my god you fucking asshole!

(**LAUREN** *disappears into the bathroom and slams the door. A moment.*)

ELLIOT. Come out of there. *(pause)* Hey. Hello? *(He knocks gently.)* Hey, come out of there and talk to me.

LAUREN. *(off)* I don't want to.

ELLIOT. You have to come out of there eventually.

LAUREN. *(off)* No I don't.

ELLIOT. You're going to live in my bathroom?

LAUREN. *(off)* I hate you.

ELLIOT. Okay. *(pause)* Or, look, you said it yourself. It was one of the first things you said to me, when we got together, that maybe we're too similar. We, you know, we do exactly the same thing, we're in the same department, we know all the same people –

(**LAUREN** *opens the door.*)

LAUREN. Oh god, and I'm going to have to see you around the fucking *department* all the time, that's right, *fuck!*

(**LAUREN** *slams the door again. A moment.*)

ELLIOT. *And,* so maybe it's too, you know...maybe we'd each be better off with someone...complementary.

(*A silence.* **LAUREN** *opens the door. A moment.*)

ELLIOT. I mean, right?

LAUREN. Who is she?

(*beat*)

ELLIOT. What?

LAUREN. Who is she that's complementary that you feel that potential again with. It's that chick *Nell,* isn't it. That undergrad?

ELLIOT. I have no idea what you're talking about.

LAUREN. There isn't somebody else.

ELLIOT. No, Jesus, I would never...

LAUREN. Well then...well then what if I hadn't gotten mad at you.

ELLIOT. What?

LAUREN. What if we hadn't had that stupid fight? Would we still be breaking up?

ELLIOT. I, what? I don't know –

LAUREN. What if instead I hadn't pushed you away before? Instead of breaking up, would we be having sex right now?

ELLIOT. I don't know. *(beat)* I guess. Probably.

LAUREN. Well then maybe we don't have to break up.

ELLIOT. Well, maybe we wouldn't have broken up *tonight*, but you were, I mean, you're right, you were mad at me because whatever I was or wasn't *doing*, you were sensing that *underneath* that I –

LAUREN. But, no, but listen, because it's, you feel these feelings that weren't available before because of your break-up with your ex-girlfriend from college have now healed and are available again.

ELLIOT. I guess.

LAUREN. And there isn't somebody else.

ELLIOT. No.

LAUREN. But so then…so then could they be available to me?

(LAUREN tries to take ELLIOT's hand but he pulls slightly away.)

ELLIOT. I don't think that's how it works.

LAUREN. What?

ELLIOT. I don't think that that's how it works.

LAUREN. So there *is* someone else.

ELLIOT. *No.* What do you – ?

LAUREN. Well, there is or there *will* be, right? Maybe you know who it is already or maybe you don't but one way or another you're going to take all that *potential* that you built up while you were with me and you're going to give it to her, and that makes me *sick*, but you know what? It's not real. It's gonna feel real at first just because she'll be new but that will run out and you'll check out again, you'll check out again, *inside,* because that's what you do, and she'll feel it, and all this will just happen again.

(beat)

ELLIOT. Well. If we're broken up. Then that really isn't any of your business. Is it.

(A moment. **LAUREN** *goes back into the bathroom and slams the door. She can be heard sobbing, off.* **ELLIOT** *sighs, crosses to his computer, sits down. He starts to type, which itself perhaps almost seems to trigger the transition to...)*

3.

(**ELLIOT**'s *place*)

(**ELLIOT** *sits at his computer, as before. A cell phone rings somewhere in the room.* **ELLIOT** *looks around. It rings again. The bathroom door opens.* **MOLLY** *comes out.*)

MOLLY. Hey, sorry.

ELLIOT. It's fine, I think, um –

MOLLY. No, I totally didn't need to pee when I left my place, and then as soon as I got here I suddenly needed to…pee. Sorry, I'll stop talking about pee now.

ELLIOT. It's fine. I think your phone is ringing.

MOLLY. What?

ELLIOT. Your phone.

MOLLY. Oh!

(**MOLLY** *heads for her bag, which is on the floor, behind something. She takes her phone, which is still ringing, out of her bag. Looks at it. Rejects the call.*)

ELLIOT. So –

MOLLY. Oh, I brought you something.

ELLIOT. What? Oh –

(**MOLLY** *puts the phone away and pulls a loaf of bread out of her bag.*)

MOLLY. As a thank you. For helping me with this. Um. Here.

ELLIOT. That's for me?

MOLLY. Yeah.

ELLIOT. That's, thanks, I really appreciate it. *(beat)* Is this a loaf of bread?

MOLLY. Yes, yeah. *(beat)* Oh I *made* it.

ELLIOT. Oh!

MOLLY. Yeah no because –

ELLIOT. That's really sweet.

MOLLY. No but it requires yeast. *(beat)* To rise, it –

ELLIOT. Oh!

MOLLY. Yeah it's a joke.

ELLIOT. Oh I get it.

MOLLY. Yeah. *(beat)* I mean you can also…eat it, I, it's *good*, I can –

ELLIOT. Yeah I, um, I will. *(beat)* Do you want me to show you how this works?

MOLLY. Please do yes.

(**ELLIOT** *goes to his desk and sits at his computer awkwardly putting the bread down to one side.* **MOLLY** *follows him. During which:*)

ELLIOT. Just yell if it gets confusing.

MOLLY. That won't be a problem.

ELLIOT. So, basically, I designed a genetic algorithm, which, I know that you're not *breeding* anything, just, all that means is that it uses the *principles* of natural selection to arrive at better and better *answers* the same way that evolution gradually produces improvements in the species, or, you know, "so fashionable theory has it," uh, but, so, yeah, *first* the algorithm randomly generates interpretations of your data and treats each as a "parent" in an initial population. And then it computes a *fitness* value for each, based on…criteria that you can set yourself, I didn't know exactly –

MOLLY. Right.

ELLIOT. And, yeah, then it sort of…"mates" them, with, um, with of course only the "fittest" getting selected, and *those* produce…"offspring" interpretations, which are then assigned fitness values of their own, and so on, generation after generation, selection, mating, offspring, periodically introducing all-important random mutation, until, after many, *many* iterations, or, you know, about two hours, it will eventually *plateau* at the most likely interpretation of your data, so, here, if you were gonna…I just labeled your unknown protein "M"? For Molly?

MOLLY. Aw.

ELLIOT. And, yeah, based on whatever factors, it will tell you how much you can trust the bonds, or *lack* thereof, between Protein M and, for now, they're labeled A, B, C –

MOLLY. *(starting to be really impressed)* Yeah, okay.

ELLIOT. And you can just keep adding more, it's…when it runs out of letters it'll just go Double-A, Double-B, Double-C, or you could just put in the protein's real… names…

(beat)

MOLLY. *Thank* you.

ELLIOT. It's no problem.

MOLLY. No, seriously, thank you, you're a lifesaver. Could I – ?

ELLIOT. Oh, of course.

*(**ELLIOT** gets up. **MOLLY** sits at the computer to play with the algorithm. **ELLIOT** watches her work for a moment. Then he goes to his kitchen area.)*

ELLIOT. Do you want something to drink?

MOLLY. Like what.

ELLIOT. Uh. *(beat)* Like, tea, or –

MOLLY. Tea?

ELLIOT. Or…whiskey?

MOLLY. Whiskey.

*(The phone in **MOLLY**'s bag rings again.)*

ELLIOT. Great. *(pause)* I think your phone is –

MOLLY. Yeah.

*(**ELLIOT** prepares two whiskeys. **MOLLY** tries to ignore her phone and focus on the computer but then, after another ring, goes to her bag again, rejects the call again, and this time puts the phone in her pocket as she goes back to the computer. During which:)*

MOLLY. I like your place.

ELLIOT. Really? I don't.

MOLLY. What? Why not?

ELLIOT. I don't know, I kind of hate how it's set up, and, like –

MOLLY. How long have you had it like this?

ELLIOT. Basically since I started grad school.

MOLLY. And how long is that?

ELLIOT. Uh, longer than I care to think about?

MOLLY. And you hate it.

ELLIOT. Yeah what I like to do is get things a certain way that I don't actually like and, instead of fixing it, just complain about it forever. It's this trick I learned from my father.

MOLLY. Yeah? He should meet my mom.

ELLIOT. Oh, does she do that?

MOLLY. No she loves *everything*. For ten minutes. You should see the emails.

ELLIOT. What about you?

MOLLY. What about me what.

ELLIOT. How long have you been here?

MOLLY. Oh I just got here.

ELLIOT. Heh. No, I meant –

MOLLY. Oh, no, so did I. This is my first semester.

ELLIOT. Oh. I mean, yeah, that's what I figured.

MOLLY. What? Why?

ELLIOT. Oh just because I only recently...noticed...you, hey, cheers!

(*Because by now* **ELLIOT** *is standing by the desk with two glasses of whiskey.*)

MOLLY. Cheers.

(*Clink.* **ELLIOT** *almost drinks. But instead of drinking* **MOLLY** *turns back to the computer and points at the screen, so* **ELLIOT** *holds off drinking as well.*)

MOLLY. Can I run it?

ELLIOT. Oh, yeah, sure, I…here.

(ELLIOT *clicks the mouse button to run the algorithm. A few moments go by.*)

MOLLY. It's not doing anything.

ELLIOT. Oh, no, it *is*, it's just it…here, if…you can watch the code run if you…

(ELLIOT *clicks his mouse again to open up the code and takes a step back.* MOLLY *watches the code run. Perhaps we see a different light playing across her face.* ELLIOT *watches* MOLLY *watch the code. A moment.*)

Yeah it's a good way to make sure something's actually… happening…

(A *few moments. Then:*)

MOLLY. (*reading what's on the screen*) "Generating Init Pop. Init Pop Full."

ELLIOT. Yeah.

MOLLY. "If A greater than B then select dot crossover A else select dot crossover B. End If."

ELLIOT. Yeah it starts out slow but stick with it, it picks up.

MOLLY. I bet. Mm!

(*Because now* MOLLY *has tried her whiskey. So* ELLIOT *drinks his.*)

ELLIOT. Yeah, it's good, right?

MOLLY. Yeah, it's really good. (*long pause*) So.

ELLIOT. Yeah. What happens now?

MOLLY. Oh. Well *now* I take this data?

ELLIOT. (*this is not what he meant*) Oh, um –

MOLLY. (*continuous*) And, well, I don't think you realize how helpful you just were because, this protein…I mean, you remember what proteins *are*, right? They're made up of amino acids, which are transcribed directly from our DNA – ?

ELLIOT. Uh, that all rings an incredibly vague bell, yeah.

MOLLY. Yeah, so they're really basic building blocks, only one level or so up from our genetic code, and they *do* everything, like, if DNA is like the architect? Proteins are the, like, little workers that actually have hammers and nails and saws and things, so when we find a *new* one, like this, which always happens accidentally, we'll be looking for something else and something we've never seen before will just pop up on a gel, when that *happens*, we try to determine what it's *for*, which, okay, enthralling, yes, I know –

ELLIOT. *(trying to seem interested as possible in all this)* I, no, it's –

MOLLY. But, okay: were you *aware* that if a three-year old child's finger is severed and you don't seal up the wound that the *entire finger* will grow back?

(beat)

ELLIOT. What if my answer to that were "yes"? How creepy would that be?

MOLLY. Heh heh.

ELLIOT. "Of course! Did you not see my *necklace* made of child fingers?" No, I did not know that. Is that true?

MOLLY. If it's just the finger*tip* it can grow back on kids as old as *ten*.

ELLIOT. *Really.*

MOLLY. There's no fingerprint and the nail will for some reason be *square* but yes.

ELLIOT. *How?*

MOLLY. That is the wrong question. The *right* question is: why does it *stop*? Why does our capacity to regenerate diminish with age? And so *that's* what our lab is studying: tissue growth, wound healing, because once you understand how these things happen naturally, or *don't*, then the process can be *synthesized* to address damage that won't heal on its own, or, "so fashionable theory has it." New skin, or bones, or *organs* even, regrown with no scarring, no fibrosis, from *inside* yourself, from your *own cells*, so no chance of rejection, the…same way you grew them all in the first place. Which would obviously be great.

ELLIOT. I, yeah, that would.

MOLLY. *But*, and this is where the yeast two-hybrid screen comes in, proteins don't actually perform their functions on their own, they all have a place as part of a larger interaction network of other proteins, a, what we call an interactome, which, if you want to visualize it, *(perhaps she draws this for him on a piece of paper)* think of the proteins as nodes, and the interactions as lines, and it all makes one big 3D map, together, in which they perform all their various functions cooperatively, so you can only find out so much about a protein in isolation before you sort of have to take her on a fishing expedition, and see if she can lead you to her friends.

ELLIOT. Bait and prey.

MOLLY. Exactly. But the problem is these screens are kind of…error prone? In that they can create conditions that never actually occur in, like, actual *nature*, like, two proteins may *bind* but never *really* appear in the same cell, or only express at different times in the life cycle, and so the bonding is meaningless, or vice-versa, a *failed* bond that's actually just dependent on some external condition I excluded from the screen, or, you know, certain proteins might just behave differently in yeast than they do in *us* –

ELLIOT. False positives and false negatives.

MOLLY. Correct, but thanks to *you*, my friend, I can now filter out the garbage, know which bonds are for real, make some predictions about the network, and then *test* them, wet, *in vivo*, by engineering an organism designed to reveal as much as possible about the function, or functions, of Protein M. Which, again, adorable.

(beat)

ELLIOT. *(genuinely fascinated by now)* And *then* what?

MOLLY. Um, *then,* depending on what I learn, I, probably give it a really literal minded-name based on its function, like integrin or versacan, and then go back, do more screens, get more data, make more predictions, do more experiments to test those, and so on, back and forth, like that, data, testing, data, testing, while other molecular biologists the world over do the same thing, gradually modeling the network more and more, until, I guess maybe, eventually, someday we'll have...mapped the whole damn thing.

ELLIOT. How close are we to *that*?

MOLLY. That depends on what you mean.

ELLIOT. By "close"?

MOLLY. By "that."

ELLIOT. Well how much of it have we mapped?

MOLLY. Less and less every day. I mean, *not* close, not the way you mean, because we keep discovering new corners we didn't even know about, so, if we're talking total human interactome? One or two percent completeness, maybe, tops? And every network is embedded hierarchically inside another, larger one, cellular, systemic, organismic, going from molecule to creature, as it were, so...I mean, that's why so many of the things our bodies do are still mysterious, because they're less *functions* than they are just *emergent properties* of this dynamic multi-layered fucking mess. So, even when the *result* is right in front of you, you're nowhere if you can't explain how it was reached. We grow and change and get sick and recover and age and die and by and large from our perspective these things just *happen.* Our bodies just *know.* So it'll be a long long time from now, if ever, before we can know with our brains all the things our bodies just already know.

*(**MOLLY** is looking at **ELLIOT.** A moment.)*

ELLIOT. What if I could help you *more?*

MOLLY. Oh, uhh –

ELLIOT. *(returning to his computer)* Or, I mean, what if I could write an algorithm that interpreted your data... better? Because *this*, all it will do is generate *probable* interpretations, *highly* probable, but, still, now that I know more what you... Before you rush off to test predictions based on *this?* What if I could write something that would give you...certainty, up front?

MOLLY. *(now it was she who was expecting something else)* Oh.

ELLIOT. I mean, I don't know *exactly* how it would work, but if you give me another few days, or more like a week? I could –

MOLLY. Right, but I'm already in your apartment. *(beat)* Right now, though. So...

ELLIOT. Oh. I mean, okay. *(pause)* Uhhh...

(**MOLLY** *and* **ELLIOT** *start to make out. They make out for a little while. Then:)*

MOLLY. Okay, can I tell you something?

ELLIOT. Sure.

MOLLY. I wasn't sure that an algorithm would be useful to me? And actually I am pleasantly surprised by how incredibly useful it turns out in fact to be? But I sort of didn't care because I just wanted an excuse to hang out with you.

ELLIOT. Can *I* tell *you* something?

MOLLY. Please.

ELLIOT. When I said something came up this afternoon so we had to meet tonight, that was a total lie, and I figured either you'd say, oh, okay, then let's just meet up tomorrow, or you'd be like, okay, what time tonight? And you said the second one? And I was like, oh, okay. It's on.

(**MOLLY** *and* **ELLIOT** *make out some more. Then:)*

MOLLY. That day, in the public cluster? I sat down at that computer because you were coming in.

ELLIOT. Actually I was leaving. I pretended to be coming in because you sat down.

(They make out some more. They move towards the bed. Then:)

MOLLY. I bought this outfit on the way here.

ELLIOT. It's so nice.

MOLLY. Thank you.

ELLIOT. "Uh, but it would blah blah blah crumpled up on my floor."

MOLLY. Heh. Heh. Mm.

*(**MOLLY**'s phone rings again. This time she rejects the call without even looking at it.)*

ELLIOT. Seriously, if it's an emergency or something, you can go ahead and –

MOLLY. It's really not.

ELLIOT. Okay.

(They make out some more. Some clothes start to come off. Then she stops him.)

MOLLY. I'm not staying over.

ELLIOT. Okay.

MOLLY. Just, I'm not going to stay over, or sleep here, or anything.

ELLIOT. Good. I'm glad.

(They make out some more. Then he stops her.)

But, wait, so you're not planning to leave until *after* the sex though, right?

*(**MOLLY** just looks at **ELLIOT**, blinking. A moment.)*

That looks like a yes.

*(**MOLLY** rolls her eyes. Then **ELLIOT** touches her face. Her arms. Just touching her.)*

MOLLY. What are you doing?

ELLIOT. I don't know. I just love this moment when you're suddenly allowed to start…touching someone? Like, you've wanted to, but of course you can't just walk up to someone and touch them, but then, suddenly, you've passed through the membrane, and you can. Like. I'd been thinking about touching you? More or less since the first time I saw you?

MOLLY. Sure. I mean, I'd...seen you too.

ELLIOT. Well, right, but for all I knew that was imaginary? Like, the idea that they might be thinking the same thing about you, you don't even let yourself entertain that possibility? And but then you're actually *here*. Like. This person I can't even believe I'm lucky enough to get to touch and she's here, she's...letting me touch her.

(beat)

MOLLY. I have to teach in the morning?

ELLIOT. Okay.

MOLLY. I have teach in the morning, undergrads, so, I'm saying, if I *do* stay? I'd need to, like, set an alarm clock for pretty early, like six thirty – ?

ELLIOT. That is not a problem.

MOLLY. Really?

ELLIOT. I don't intend for us to sleep at *all*.

MOLLY. Heh.

ELLIOT. Oh not because we'll be fooling around. Just because after we're done I'll keep you awake with long boring stories about my family because physical intimacy will have created the illusion of emotional intimacy. Come here.

MOLLY. No really if you could set it now.

ELLIOT. Oh –

MOLLY. I just don't want us to forget.

ELLIOT. No, yeah, okay.

*(**ELLIOT** sets his alarm clock. During which:)*

MOLLY. Just, I co-teach, with this other grad student, and I'm *chronically* late, and it's important he not hate me, so –

ELLIOT. It's not a problem.

MOLLY. He gives genetic diseases to mice so there's no telling what he'd do to me.

ELLIOT. I teach in the morning too.

MOLLY. Oh okay.

ELLIOT. Yeah.

MOLLY. Kind of sucks, doesn't it.

(*ELLIOT checks the alarm two or three more times before turning away from it.*)

ELLIOT. Uh, it can. When they're passive idiots. But once in a while…I've got this one *incredibly* sharp kid this semester, she –

MOLLY. Hey come here.

(*ELLIOT goes there. More making out. Then ELLIOT struggles with whatever is keeping MOLLY's pants closed. He peers at her pants carefully.*)

ELLIOT. Huh.

MOLLY. It's, oh, you have to, if you… See?

ELLIOT. Oh yeah. It's, see real world objects…I can't…

(*MOLLY does not struggle at all with ELLIOT's pants. Soon ELLIOT and MOLLY are both in their underwear. A moment.*)

Hold on.

MOLLY. What.

(*ELLIOT goes around and starts turning off the various lights.*)

You don't want to see me?

ELLIOT. Oh, no, just. Mood lighting.

MOLLY. I want to see you.

(*The only light remaining is the lamp next to the bed, which ELLIOT was just reaching for. Instead, he leaves this on and reaches for MOLLY again.*)

MOLLY. I don't normally do this.

ELLIOT. Oh. Okay.

MOLLY. Just so you know.

ELLIOT. Okay. *(beat)* Why do girls always say that?

MOLLY. What?

ELLIOT. What.

MOLLY. "Girls"? "Always"?

ELLIOT. *(overlapping)* Oh, no, I just –

MOLLY. Cause invoking other girls right now isn't really, like…the best idea…

ELLIOT. *(overlapping)* No, please, I'm not, I don't mean… *(beat)* I just… Not that there have been…in my *extremely limited* experience. At a certain moment. Girls have a tendency to say. "I don't normally do this."

MOLLY. Okay.

ELLIOT. Which can only mean one of two things. That I'm just so *appealing* that I am an exception to the otherwise intractable courtship rules of the entire female population. Which let's table for the moment as unlikely. *Or.* They're lying. Which I would prefer also not to believe. So I was just wondering. As someone who has just now actually said it. If you had any insight into what it really means.

(beat)

MOLLY. I think that you've failed to consider a third possibility.

ELLIOT. What's that.

MOLLY. That, because not only do they normally not *sleep* with someone *right away*, but, with most people, they don't do it *ever*, that it's not a lie. It's just that, with someone where they know they're *going* to want to? They figure that they might as well start, like, immediately. So it's not that you're *in general* so appealing either. It just looks that way from your perspective because your sampling size self-selects for people who have *already decided* to sleep, specifically, with you.

(beat)

ELLIOT. You're right.

MOLLY. I know.

ELLIOT. I made a derivation error.

(*The phone rings in the pocket of* **MOLLY**'s *discarded pants. A moment.*)

MOLLY. If that's what it's…called… I'm going to turn that off. (*She goes to her phone and turns it off. Then:*) Hold on a second.

ELLIOT. What.

(**MOLLY** *heads for the bathroom*)

MOLLY. I, um. I have to pee again.

ELLIOT. It's the whisky.

MOLLY. No I think I'm just nervous.

(**MOLLY** *exits.* **ELLIOT** *sits on the bed and waits. He grins and laughs slightly, basking in the awesomeness of this moment. Then he turns off the remaining light. Moves clothes off his bed. There is still light from his computer screen, so* **ELLIOT** *gets up and goes to turn it off. Light from the street through windows is all that's left. And* **ELLIOT** *is still in the middle of the room when* **MOLLY** *emerges from the bathroom, naked. Naked in streetlight and moonlight. A moment.*)

MOLLY. Hi.

ELLIOT. Hi.

MOLLY. Sorry, too much? Too soon?

ELLIOT. What? No. No no no. No, uh…

(**ELLIOT** *removes his remaining clothing and tosses it aside. A moment.*)

MOLLY. I see what you mean.

ELLIOT. What.

MOLLY. About the light.

(*They stand looking at each other, across the bed, for a moment. In the near dark, they look blue. Then they slip into the bed from opposite sides.* **ELLIOT** *moves to*

MOLLY *but she stops him. She reaches down below the covers and peers after her hand. A moment.)*

ELLIOT. Uh, what are you doing?

MOLLY. Having sex without examining the genitals is like biting into a piece of fruit without looking at it. *(pause)* Okay.

ELLIOT. Okay?

MOLLY. Yeah. Just yell if it gets confusing.

*(**MOLLY** and **ELLIOT** intertwine...transition...the sound of a ringing phone, as heard by the caller, takes us into...)*

4.

(the front steps of a university housing building)

*(**DON** is here, holding a cell phone to his ear. He waits. Listens. Then, at last:)*

DON. Hey I don't know where you are. *(beat)* Which is, that's fine, in…principle, I'm not, you are a free… person. Just. I'm worried about you. So call me. *(beat)* I mean maybe your phone is just off. But it seems like it's ringing and you're not… I mean, if you're *angry* at me, or, if I did something *wrong,* I'd rather you just talked to me or told me instead of disappearing, but, which, I mean if your phone is just off, then ignore that part, it's not a big deal, I just meant, mainly I'm worried. Because you're also not home either, so, or, if you are, just, okay, I'm on the street in front of your place right now? Not in a creepy way, I'm just…telling you where I am. Or, that's not, look, I know that I've been busy lately, okay? So I'm sorry if… *(beat)* You know what? Just ignore this entire message. And call me whenever. If you want. Or don't, I'll just…see you in the department. *(beat)* This is Don. *(beat)* Bye.

*(**DON** hangs up. He does not feel good about how that went. Sits on the steps. Thinks. Shudders. Takes out the phone again. Scrolls through some numbers. Dials again. A phone rings.)*

*(Lights up on the Computer Science departmental office. The phone on the front desk is ringing, unattended. It rings again. **LAUREN** walks by the desk. Stops and turns back when she hears the phone ring. Looks around for anyone. It rings again.)*

*(**DON** is about to hang up. **LAUREN** answers the phone.)*

LAUREN. Computer Science.

DON. Hi, this is Professor Davis, from Molecular Biology?

LAUREN. Okay.

(beat)

DON. Uh, yeah, one of my grad students, my, uh, my advisee, had a meeting scheduled this evening? With one of *your* grad students? And I was just wondering whether she was still there.

LAUREN. There's...*no* one here.

DON. Well could you maybe check?

*(**LAUREN** looks around for a second, perfunctorily.)*

LAUREN. There's no one here.

DON. Well, if the departmental secretary is still there, then maybe –

LAUREN. Um, I'm not a *secretary?* I'm a graduate student.

DON. Well, whoever you are, you're *there,* so –

LAUREN. Yeah but no one *else* is here because it's *night.*

DON. Okay but could you please just actually – ?

LAUREN. MB and B is one floor down, why don't you just come up here yourself?

(beat)

DON. I'm not there.

LAUREN. Yeah! *No* one is!

DON. Okay, okay, look, I'm sorry, just... Her name is Molly and she was supposedly meeting with this guy Elliot and I just want to know if they're still there. Please. *(long pause)* Hello?

LAUREN. Uh, no.

DON. What?

LAUREN. No. He's...not, there's... *(beat)* No one's here.

*(**LAUREN** hangs up the phone. She sits down on the desk. She is shaking.)*

DON. Hello? *(pause)* Hello? *(pause)* Are you there?

(...transition...)

5.

*(**ELLIOT**'s place)*

*(Pre-dawn light through the window. **MOLLY** and **ELLIOT** are in bed together, after.)*

ELLIOT. Well my Dad's a high school math teacher? So I guess it runs in the family, or it's what was, you know, *modeled,* or both.

MOLLY. That must be nice.

ELLIOT. What.

MOLLY. To have, like, an affinity, with your Dad –

ELLIOT. Yeah, you'd think. Or, I mean, it is. In a way. But he's also always giving me suggestions and advice about my work to which there's kind of no proper way to respond? Like, if I treat his ideas like they're coming from a peer, he gets offended by how gruff I am when I dismiss them? But if I treat them like they're coming from my *father,* and dismiss them *gently,* he feels condescended to, so –

MOLLY. What about when you don't dismiss his ideas?

ELLIOT. Heh. That's funny. *(beat)* Or, you're right, I mean, I think he wanted...but instead... *(pause)* What about you?

MOLLY. What about me what. Oh, I don't know, I mean, my mom's not, like, a biology teacher or anything. She's kind of a hippie, actually. Like, she and I moved a lot, and she's all about hiking and being in the woods and, like, the earth, and crystals and things? Which is not me. That's not me. But sometimes I think I'm, like, the science *version* of that? Like I sort of rejected what I saw as her, like, flakiness? But, like, secretly, even secretly from myself? I'm actually into exactly the same stuff as she is, just in the most, like, rigorous way possible.

ELLIOT. Heh. *(beat)* The last girl that I dated had this incredibly fraught relationship with her parents, like, they would talk on the phone *every day*, and she would *always* get off in *tears*, it was this, like, constant battle of justifying herself, everything she did, and this was not, by the way, a, like, wayward or unsuccessful person, but they somehow always made her cry about how she was disappointing them, or... And I'd just be like: maybe back off talking to them *every single day*. But she could not stop.

MOLLY. Huh. *(beat)* When was that?

ELLIOT. Umm...

MOLLY. What, recently?

ELLIOT. Uhhh –

MOLLY. Hold on, did I, like, *steal* you from somebody, or – ?

ELLIOT. What? No! No, you... No.

MOLLY. Really?

ELLIOT. Or, so what if you did? Isn't that kind of awesome for you?

MOLLY. What? Ew! No!

ELLIOT. Huh. I find that fascinating. See, for me –

MOLLY. So I *did* steal you.

ELLIOT. No! No, it was... *(beat)* It was just this *rebound* that went on longer than it should have, it...needed to end.

MOLLY. And it was not because of me.

ELLIOT. No it was not because of you. *(beat)* Except for that it totally *was* insofar as you...opened my eyes to what else was out there, okay?

MOLLY. Okay. *(long pause)* So is there really a way to know, up front, for sure?

ELLIOT. What?

MOLLY. To fix the algorithm, like you said, to –

ELLIOT. Oh!

MOLLY. To interpret the data better.

ELLIOT. Yeah, no, I thought... *(beat)* Sorry, I thought we'd agreed that was a ruse upon which we'd mutually conspired to get each other into bed.

MOLLY. Well right but also you said that, given some more time – ?

ELLIOT. Yeah, I, no, I may have *said* that? But, in the spirit of, um, post-coital honesty? It might not actually be what you'd call "possible." I mean, I could *try*, I could absolutely write something. But by the time it was done running we would both be dead and so would our children. *(beat)* I mean the children we might someday have. *(beat)* With *anybody*. Not necessarily with each other. *(beat)* I mean not with each other. *(beat)* What I'm saying is I think it might actually be an example of the TSP.

MOLLY. What's the TSP?

ELLIOT. Well, trying to produce a definitively correct interpretation of your data.

MOLLY. No, what do you mean "The TSP"?

ELLIOT. Oh! The Traveling Salesman Problem.

MOLLY. What's the Traveling Salesman Problem?

ELLIOT. Seriously?

MOLLY. Yeah. What.

ELLIOT. No, I'm just...so excited that I get to *explain* it, uh...here. Okay. So. An *algorithm* is a set of instructions, right? A script, in code, like, "if *this* then choose *that* or else some *other* thing," which, when *followed*, will complete a task, in, given the computational speed of machines, *much* less time than it would take you or me, using only our pathetic brains. But. *Some* problems remain intractable. For instance: the Traveling Salesman Problem. Which goes like this: *(By now he is at his whiteboard, wearing only boxers and a t shirt.)* Imagine you're a Traveling Salesman, from some hometown *(He writes "HOME" on the board.)* who needs to visit a certain number of cities, X, *(He writes "X =".)* and then return home, and you want to do this, naturally, while covering the shortest possible distance.

MOLLY. Okay...

(beat)

ELLIOT. No, that's it, that's the problem.

MOLLY. *(overlapping)* Oh, that's it?

ELLIOT. Yeah.

MOLLY. But that's, but it's...I mean, do I *fly*, or – ?

ELLIOT. Doesn't matter. Assume straight lines.

MOLLY. Well then don't I just measure the distance between each city and add up the total distance for each route and then pick the lowest number?

ELLIOT. Yes. *Or* you could write an *algorithm* which could do that *for* you.

MOLLY. Okay so then –

ELLIOT. *But.* An algorithm that does that, that checks every possible option, or that, what we say is, produces the entire solution space and traverses it, that's called an exhaustive search or 'brute force' algorithm, and if the Salesman, let's say he's visiting three cities...

*(**ELLIOT** completes "X =" with "3" and then draws three dots, labeling them "A" "B" and "C".)*

...A, B, and C, it'll go *(He draws the paths quickly.)* ABC, ACB, CBA, it'll try all the routes, and the only actual *math* involved is, like you said, it's *addition*, and, sure, for *three* cities there's only six possible routes and the problem is trivial, but for four cities...there's twenty-four possible routes...and for five, there's a hundred and twenty, and, I mean you can begin to see how steep the curve is, it's a factorial, *every time* you add a city the *number of possible routes* goes up *exponentially*, so the *real* problem turns out to be the *rate* at which the *complexity increases*. Like, for eleven cities? Which is not that many cities? The number of possible routes is around forty million. For fourteen cities, which is still not that many cities? It's close to ninety billion. So for fifty, or a hundred, or a thousand cities – ?

MOLLY. Or protein pairs.

ELLIOT. – exactly? There aren't *words* for numbers that big. And, faced with that, a brute force algorithm will just freeze. It will just sit there and do nothing. And give you no answer at all. *(beat)* Or, okay, that's not accurate, that's not what's happening, what's *really* happening is it's not *frozen?* It's *thinking.* It's just that it will take *so long* to *finish* thinking, like, literally *thousands* of *centuries,* it might as *well* be frozen, from, like, the perspective of an actual human lifespan, so the problem is *solvable,* it's just not solvable in what we call polynomial time, in, like, a human scale of time, as opposed to exponential time, where some immortal being with infinite patience could be like, "What's the big deal? Just wait a hundred million years and the answer will pop right out." Or it could be solved by some kind of magical, nondeterministic computer, that at every crossroads makes an essentially random guess, but does this with perfect luck, like, hm, left turn, right turn, and every single choice is automatically correct, that would work too. But we're not immortal. And we can't make random guesses with perfect luck. And so there isn't, we can't, like… Do you, are you with me so far, or – ?

MOLLY. Yeah, yeah, no, keep going.

ELLIOT. Yeah but does this like actually *interest* you, or – ?

MOLLY. Yes very much.

ELLIOT. Really?

MOLLY. You listened to my whole thing about protein interaction networks.

ELLIOT. True but that was back *before* I knew if I was going to see you *naked* later.

MOLLY. And by the same token *I* am now trying to *remain* appealing *after* sex.

(beat)

ELLIOT. Okay so obviously exhaustive search is pretty inelegant and clumsy, not to mention requires like a giant room full of enormous computers, so what you *really* do is you look at your underlying code and start to complicate it, you use pruning techniques, branch and bound techniques, ways of *honing* the algorithm, basically, so that it doesn't need to check *every single possibility*, like, it can dismiss obviously stupid ideas, going back and forth between cities that are really far apart for no reason, but even *that* won't work, not at high enough values of X. So you could *also* try a different category of algorithm all together, like the genetic algorithm I wrote for you, or some other kind of probabilistic or heuristic algorithm, because what *they* do is they *optimize*, they sort of say, "Hey, you know what? I don't need the *best possible* route. I just want a *really really good* one." But *that* method only gives you an answer in the sense that you changed the definition of what 'answer' is. You settled, in other words. So what's *really* required is an insight so profound into the deep structure of the problem that it gives rise to a new kind of algorithm, of unprecedented elegance, some, probably, some combination of brute force *and* heuristics, that searches *and* optimizes, embracing compromise *en route* to a *kind* of certainty, thereby unearthing a real genuine solution to this problem. *Or* for someone to prove, definitively? That no such algorithm exists. And in the fifty-odd years since the TSP was first described, *no* one, *anywhere*, has *ever* been able to do *either* of those things.

MOLLY. It's unsolved.

ELLIOT. It's the most important unsolved problem in all of Computer Science. It's *one* of the most important unsolved problems in all of mathematics. It has implications for, well, business, of course, it's a real world problem for, like, actual *salesmen*, on, like, an *industrial* scale, but it also turns out to be *analogous* to *hundreds* of other problems, in game theory, language theory, apparently in biology, to basically *any problem* of *satisfiability*, of exponentially branching choices that can be solved in our lifetimes seemingly only by random guesses made with perfect luck. Your nodes may be cities or proteins or...something else...but the problem remains the same. And because these NP problems, these Nondeterministic Polynomial Time problems, are all reducible to, or derivable from, one another? Because they're what we call NP-Complete? What this *means* is, if you solve *any one* of them? You'll actually have solved them *all*. And this is known as the Theory of NP-Completeness. And it's what I'm working on. Pretty much all the time.

(*beat*)

MOLLY. Have you done this before?

ELLIOT. What?

MOLLY. This little presentation.

ELLIOT. Well, yeah, of course, in class, or, I mean it's –

MOLLY. No have you done this before in more or less this context.

(*beat*)

ELLIOT. Um –

MOLLY. I knew it! This is your A material!

ELLIOT. No –

MOLLY. It totally *is!* You say this to *all* the girls!

ELLIOT. I, what, I talk about computational intractability?

MOLLY. I bet you do!

ELLIOT. And that gets everybody right into the sack.

MOLLY. I bet it does! I bet they're like, "Brute force? Oh, Elliot, tell me more."

ELLIOT. Look at it this way: would you rather be *unworthy* of my A material?

MOLLY. Oh I don't know. What does *that* look like?

ELLIOT. That's where, as soon as we're finished I just go, "So... How are you getting home?"

MOLLY. Heh heh heh.

ELLIOT. By the way, how *are* you getting home? Should I, like, call a car, or – ?

MOLLY. Shut the fuck up.

ELLIOT. I can walk you as far as the door.

MOLLY. And they say chivalry is dead.

(A moment. Then **MOLLY** *starts to get out of bed.)*

ELLIOT. Oh god, I was totally kidding, please stay.

MOLLY. No, I know.

ELLIOT. Yeah, no, I would never send you out there now. It's Winter.

MOLLY. No, I, haha, but, no, I just have to pee again. I don't know what's wrong with me.

ELLIOT. Maybe you're pregnant.

(beat)

MOLLY. That's not funny.

ELLIOT. It was a joke.

MOLLY. I know. But that joke's not funny.

ELLIOT. No, yeah, but: keep in mind that we had sex like an *hour* ago, so, even if you *were* pregnant, you wouldn't *already* be having, like, physiological –

MOLLY. Explaining it more does not help!

ELLIOT. Right, but the *joke*, I'm saying, was that –

MOLLY. Elliot. No woman. Anywhere. Ever. Since long before records of such things were kept. Has ever found that joke funny.

ELLIOT. Okay.

MOLLY. Okay.

*(***MOLLY*** turns away, as if to get up. But, then, instead she just sort of stares off into space for a second. Worried? Sad? Anyway, she doesn't stand. A silence.)*

ELLIOT. Yeah that was a really bad joke, I'm sorry –

MOLLY. Oh, no, it's totally not that, I just... I was just thinking.

ELLIOT. Oh. Well *that* doesn't sound like a good idea.

MOLLY. No, just... *(Beat. Then, quietly:)* I feel sort of like I tricked you.

ELLIOT. Oh. *(beat)* In, uhh…in what way.

MOLLY. Into thinking that I'm…happy. Or good. Or any fun to be around.

ELLIOT. Oh. *(beat)* Except. I *am* having fun. So…

*(A moment. Then **MOLLY** gets up and moves towards the bathroom.)*

But you aren't leaving, right?

MOLLY. What?

ELLIOT. You're gonna stay?

MOLLY. Yeah. I'm gonna stay.

*(**MOLLY** exits to the bathroom. A moment. Then **ELLIOT** looks at his whiteboard, where, in the midst of all the lines and letters and numbers, is the word: "HOME." Intermission.)*

6.

*(**MOLLY***'s lab)*

*(**MOLLY** is standing here facing **DON**. She is holding the Petri dish she showed to **ELLIOT** in Scene One. Other Petri dishes full of the results of various other hybrid screens, successful and unsuccessful, are all over the counter behind her. There is also a computer somewhere in the lab.)*

MOLLY. So you were right. I mean, you were right, to be worried, at first. Because, originally the...data *was* pretty messy, pretty difficult to read. But it turns out it's not a problem because this, I guess, algorithm? Once I worked out how to use it, could clean the data *up* enough that...I mean, not *completely*? That's impossible, apparently? For...very long and complex reasons? But enough to know where the real pathways likely are.

(beat)

DON. Sounds *great.*

MOLLY. Yeah and so I also wanted to just thank you for... pushing me to have such high standards. Because otherwise I might have stayed just, you know –

DON. *(overlapping)* You are very welcome.

MOLLY. Kind of stuck just where I was.

DON. Well that is my job.

MOLLY. Well, but, yeah, so... *(A moment. Then, glancing at the other Petri dishes:)* So what do we do with these now, do we wash them all, or – ?

DON. Oh, no no.

MOLLY. Well, but, for reuse.

DON. No, what do you – ? Molly, those will never be sterile again. We'll just order new ones.

MOLLY. Oh. Okay.

DON. Yeah, you're...not in college anymore.

MOLLY. Um. Okay. *(She puts the petri dish down among the others. A moment. Then she steels herself, and:)* So, okay, so I should tell you –

DON. That you're seeing this guy?

MOLLY. Um –

DON. This algorithm guy, this: Elliot? You're *involved* with him now, yeah?

MOLLY. I mean, I don't know if I'd say we're... *involved*, exac –

DON. No, it's, look, it's *fine*, I... Listen, this? You and me? This thing was *bound* to end, at some point, right? It was... I mean, it probably shouldn't have *started* in the *first* place, it's, you know, very... And so now that this happened, well, then, great, you know? It's probably for the best.

MOLLY. Oh. Um: okay.

DON. Yeah, so...do not worry about it.

MOLLY. Okay. Yeah. *(beat)* Except, in your voicemail? You seemed –

DON. Voicemail.

MOLLY. Yeah you left me, like, this *message*, where you sounded kind of – ?

DON. Huh.

MOLLY. Yeah.

DON. I do not remember that.

MOLLY. What? Really?

DON. I, yeah, no, I've been... You know what? I've been taking this, like, cold medication? And it makes me kind of... I mean that stuff's basically speed, so, who knows *what* I... I mean, haha, *sorry* about that. But no. Yeah. No.

MOLLY. Okay.

DON. Okay.

MOLLY. In that case can we talk about what's next?

DON. Of course!

*(During the following, **MOLLY** heads over to the computer in the lab and brings up what are, presumably, the results of running **ELLIOT**'s genetic algorithm.)*

MOLLY. Well, because, according to *this?* Protein M binds to…: collagen, integrin, fibronectin, thrombospondin, myosin, perlacan, *several* growth factors –

DON. Wow, quite the molecular hussy.

MOLLY. 'Scuse me?

DON. And, I'm sorry: "Protein M?"

MOLLY. What? Oh –

DON. You named it after yourself?

MOLLY. No, *I*…didn't, he…

DON. Oh I see. Cute. Go on?

(beat)

MOLLY. I will rename it after its function with a nice vowel-n suffix like we do –

DON. I'm –

MOLLY. – once I know exactly what that function *is*.

DON. I am sure you will.

MOLLY. So! What I'd like to do is a straight knockout. In mice. I thought about RNA interference, but people are getting great results now by just injecting damaged genes directly into mouse gonads –

DON. I know what a straight knockout is.

MOLLY. – and, yeah, hoping for germ line transmission –

DON. I know how they work.

MOLLY. Well so then that's what I would like to do. *(beat)* Yeah, I'm sorry, what do *you* think?

DON. Well, first of all, I think, just slow down a second there, okay? Just slowww down.

MOLLY. Okay.

DON. Yeah. *(beat)* Okay, for one thing? You can't really *do* knockouts in this area. The phenotypes are too severe, you'll…kill the mice.

MOLLY. Well, but –

DON. Secondly. Mice are expensive. Like: an order of magnitude more expensive than flies or worms or –

MOLLY. Franklin uses mice.

DON. Franklin's been here longer.

MOLLY. My results won't mean as much in anything but mice.

DON. Well, but, regardless, most importantly, um: what makes you so sure that this rather prodigious list of interaction partners is *accurate?*

MOLLY. Oh, well, because the algorithm –

DON. Heh, yeah, okay, um… *(beat)* Look, it's *great* you tried to mitigate false positives. That's *great.* And I know that these computational approaches can be very…flashy and impressive in the short term, that is, hey: that's why they're so fashionable right now, yeah? But, as the basis for devoting significant departmental resources, "because a computer said so" leaves, for me, something to be desired.

MOLLY. So…what are you saying?

DON. I'm saying either the band is on the gel, so to speak, or else it's not. I'm saying if you have to use statistical analysis to *make* your data say certain things then your data is itself unreliable. I'm saying that if you wish to move on to genetic perturbations of *any* kind, then you should go back, and do more screens, and get these results for *real*, because, in the end, in my experience, nothing takes the place of a person, in a room, just putting in the time, not even a big fancy algorithm, okay? Okay.

(DON crosses away. MOLLY is not looking at him. Then, as in scene two, the computer starts to get a tiny bit noisy, as though stuck, working hard on something. MOLLY immediately hits whatever buttons are necessary to stop it. She turns toward DON.)

MOLLY. You told me I was brave.

DON. What?

MOLLY. It was one of the first things you said to me, when you took me on, you said that you thought I was brave, and –

DON. Yes, that's right.

MOLLY. And that that was important because the longer we *do* this kind of thing the harder it gets not to fall into certain patterns that can stunt our progress. That the cure for that is being brave.

DON. I remember saying those things, yes.

MOLLY. Okay, but in this case for some reason...?

(beat)

DON. Molly, if there's something you'd like to say – ?

MOLLY. I, well, okay, I just question whether you're being impartial.

DON. Why, because of your personal life?

MOLLY. Because of your connection to my personal life, yes.

DON. Keep your voice down. *(beat)* I told you that's a non-issue.

MOLLY. What if I don't *believe* you?

DON. Oh because there couldn't *possibly* be problems with your work and so it has to be some kind of *bias*?

MOLLY. It's not *what* you're saying about my work, Don, it's how. It's the tone of condescension and barely concealed hostility which –

DON. Uh, well, maybe I *sound* that way because *you're* not being impartial.

MOLLY. What?

DON. That's right. Maybe the *problem* here is that you're so excited about your new *boyfriend* and –

MOLLY. I, he's not my...! Jesus...

DON. *(continuous)* – about how he has all the *answers* that your judgment as a scientist is clouded, because frankly, Molly, if I were you, I wouldn't be so quick to waste ten thousand dollars worth of grant money in your first semester *here* provided that your plan is to *remain* here very *long.*

MOLLY. Is that a *threat?*

DON. It is *advice.* In that you are my *advisee.*

MOLLY. I see. And do you think giving that sort of advice to your advisee right after she stops *sleeping* with you is really a recipe for career longevity yourself there, Don?

(*beat*)

DON. You know what? Let's just slow this right back down a second here, okay? Let's just slowww down. (*beat*) Why don't we say this: write up what you'd like to do, as a proposal, and I will take it under –

MOLLY. (*overlapping*) No, I think under the circumstances? (*beat*) I think it would be best if I had a different faculty adviser from now on.

(*beat*)

DON. That's not how it works.

MOLLY. What?

DON. There's an official...You have to go through the department and reque –

MOLLY. Well so I will do that then.

DON. If that's what you'd like to do.

MOLLY. It is.

DON. But what I think you'll find is that a similar philosophy to mine obtains more or less department wide.

(*A moment.* **MOLLY** *is about to say something else when her phone rings. A moment. It rings again.*)

DON. Go ahead, don't keep him waiting.

MOLLY. It's, that's not funny, it's not even...

(**MOLLY** *looks at her phone. Oh. It totally is* **ELLIOT** *calling. It rings again.*)

DON. It's all right, I'll go.

MOLLY. We're not finished.

DON. *(already walking out)* Yes we are.

MOLLY. Don –

DON. No, you should really call him back. I mean you don't want to burn *that* bridge too, do you? Not until you've worked out someplace *else* to go. Am I right? Molly? *(beat)* Good luck with your work.

*(**DON** exits. **MOLLY** stands there for second. Then she realizes her phone has long since stopped ringing and puts it down. It instantly rings again. A beat. Then **MOLLY** answers.)*

MOLLY. Hello?

*(**ELLIOT** enters the lab, phone to his ear. He looks extremely disheveled.)*

ELLIOT. Hi, sorry, it's just me, hi.

MOLLY. Oh. Hi.

ELLIOT. Is this a bad time?

MOLLY. Kind of, yeah.

ELLIOT. Oh. *(A beat. Then, lowering the phone:)* See this is why I hate the phone? You never know if people –

MOLLY. Elliot, what do you want?

ELLIOT. Um, well –

*(An email arrives on the computer with an "arrival" noise. **MOLLY** goes to check it.)*

MOLLY. Hold on.

ELLIOT. That's from me.

MOLLY. What?

ELLIOT. I just sent that.

MOLLY. When?

ELLIOT. Just now, before I called you twice, and also ran downstairs.

*(**MOLLY** has by now opened the email. She doesn't know what she's looking at.)*

MOLLY. Elliot, what *is* this?

ELLIOT. Well, it started...I was trying to help you. Not to...read your data better, I was still thinking that was impossible, but to, maybe, as you move forward to your next experiments? Might it not be *helpful* to have a computer model first, an...algorithmic simulation of the network that you're studying, with all the proteins you already understand doing their thing, and your unknown protein in the mix, so that you could make predictions and then test them I guess, dry, um, *in silico*, but *then*, I *realized*... Okay: when we think of the Traveling Salesman Problem what we always think about is one salesman, trying to choose a route. The nodes are destination points and the lines are paths he moves along. But *what* if... What if the nodes aren't points but more like bounded areas separated from the space around them by a sort of *membrane*. Like a cell. Each with its own ability to make choices as though there's a...salesman in *every* city, or like every city *is* a salesman, or... Sorry, I haven't left my office in almost four days? So I'm a little –

MOLLY. No it's fine.

ELLIOT. And what if you could then input, or, I guess, *inject*, something like the Traveling Salesman Problem, into each cell, as a propositional formula, a...question for it to answer, and what if those cells could then multiply, exponentially, to keep pace with exhaustive search, while also being probabilistic, because every cell is making its own random choices every time it runs, with each one finally, sort of, *excreting* its answer into the surrounding area, which, rather than there being set paths *between* them, would just be this, sort of, larger matrix they all share, in which all their answers are *combined*, and which is itself surrounded by another, larger membrane, which is itself just one cell among many, and so on, each level embedded hierarchically inside the next, such that their combined work gets passed up, and up, going from molecule to creature, as it were, until some outermost skin membrane, is reached, and one, sort of, *ultimate* answer is sent out, one *collective* answer, arrived at through a combination of brute force and heuristics, non-deterministically, but with perfect luck. What if the algorithm...*is* an organism?

MOLLY. You should *try* that.

ELLIOT. *(pointing to the computer screen)* I *did*. I *did* try it. And I think there's something wrong with it, because... Eventually, that answer *does*...it just...*comes out!* As an, I guess, emergent property of this dynamic multi-layered fucking mess. It just happens. The algorithm just... knows. *(beat)* And so there must be something *wrong* with it because if there's not, if I just built something that can solve an NP-Complete problem like the TSP inside polynomial time, well, then that means...

MOLLY. That actually you've solved them all.

(beat)

ELLIOT. Is...there a chair, anywhere – ?

MOLLY. I, can I *see* it?

ELLIOT. Uh, yeah, that's why I sent it to you. Here.

*(They go back over to the computer. **ELLIOT** opens something and **MOLLY** looks at it. Lights plays across their faces from the screen. It seems to be beautiful. Then:)*

MOLLY. Oh.

ELLIOT. Right? I'd been working on this thing, non-stop, for years. And the right idea came as soon as I left it alone and worked on something else.

MOLLY. Isn't that just always how it goes.

*(They stare at the screen...**ELLIOT** takes **MOLLY**'s hand...transition...during the transition, **DON** and **LAUREN** cross paths, in a hallway somewhere perhaps... **LAUREN** glances at **DON** as she passes him...**DON** looks back and checks out **LAUREN**...she continues off, oblivious...**DON** stops, turns, and follows **LAUREN** off...)*

7.

(MOLLY's place)

(One big space, desk, bed, kitchen, doors. A laptop computer on the desk. Afternoon light. **ELLIOT** *and* **MOLLY** *are here, maybe both sitting on the bed, but in any case half-dressed, as though they had sex a little while ago and are in what they threw on after.)*

ELLIOT. Well we all know what usually happens with something like this, right? We all know how it usually goes. For a while it seems like you got everything right, finally, like everything is perfect, and then suddenly some...unforeseen issue arises out of nowhere, and you're just like, oh god, no, not this again.

MOLLY. Right.

ELLIOT. And in this case I really do not want for that to happen.

MOLLY. Right, no. I mean, me either.

ELLIOT. Not with you and me.

MOLLY. Right, no.

(beat)

ELLIOT. So then, okay, can I tell you something?

MOLLY. Sure.

ELLIOT. And allow me to preface this by saying that the *reason* I am telling you this is, like I said, because I do not want for it to happen? But I have had, historically? This...problem. Where as soon a, like, romantic situation is established, like, officially? I start to get this....feeling, this, like...persistent feeling, of, like, nagging discomfort, or, hm, like these *waves* of... anxiety? Or paralysis? Or, just, *obligation*, just this feeling of my whole life being *circumscribed* in this deadening way that fills me with overwhelming dread, with this, just, sadness, this, just, heavy choking sadness that turns me into this, like, shell of a person who is not capable of joy, only suffering. *(beat)* And, you know, maybe I try to sort of ride that feeling out, and see if it will go away, but it never does, until, one way or another, the whole thing falls apart, about which I feel secretly relieved.

MOLLY. Okay.

ELLIOT. And, again, I do not feel that happening *here*, like, it does not seem to be happening in this case? But just to, like, preempt it or, I guess, ward it off? I thought I'd put it out there.

MOLLY. Okay. *(beat)* I mean, yeah, let's keep an eye on all that, shall we?

ELLIOT. Um, okay, yeah.

(beat)

MOLLY. Yeah, okay, can *I* tell *you* something?

ELLIOT. Sure!

MOLLY. Because *I* have had, historically, a problem, as well? Where I'll be with someone, and then just... disappear? Like, one day, suddenly you will just never hear from me again? And you'll be like, "What the fuck just happened? *(beat)* ...happened...happened... happened?" *(beat)* Those were the echoes of your question going unanswered –

ELLIOT. *(overlapping)* Yeah I got it.

MOLLY. Which, I mean, I sort of...*just* did to someone, actually?

ELLIOT. *Oh.*

MOLLY. Why, is that "awesome" for you?

ELLIOT. Kind of.

MOLLY. Gross.

ELLIOT. Probably.

MOLLY. Okay well, the point is, I think the reason it keeps happening is that I've been sort of...*using* things? To help me move on from something else, from...just this guy who... Just that first person with whom you can envision having, like, a home?

ELLIOT. *(chipper, "I totally get it!")* Her name was Katie!

MOLLY. *("Awesome!")* His was Clark!

ELLIOT. What happened?

MOLLY. It doesn't matter. The point is, when I came here...I mean, it was to go to school, of course it was, but it was also to...start over a little? Which worked. In a way. Like, when things are pretty busy, and I'm preoccupied, or sometimes you just *forget*, I *feel* like I'm okay. But then also sometimes, when things get quiet enough, it feels like nothing else has happened to me since. Like nothing real has happened in my life since. Are you, does this make any sense, or – ?

ELLIOT. No, yeah. it does.

MOLLY. Yeah, but, is this, like, really boring to you, or – ?

ELLIOT. No, go on. Tell me.

MOLLY. Because this is what it's like. It's like you walk off down the road. And you think you're making all this progress. And then you stop, and look down, and you're like, oh: he *is* the road. And so then the *question* becomes: what am I supposed to *do*? Like, does that mean I shouldn't try again, or that I definitely *should*, like, right *away*? Like, is *waiting* the answer, or is it the *problem* because the *answer* is *not* waiting? And if I don't know then how am I supposed to tell somebody else I want to be with him and mean it? And, if I *do* like someone, and if that makes me forget my sadness for a while, then does that mean that that person makes me happy? Or does that just mean that, once that fades, once he's not *useful* anymore, for like masking or replacing all my pain, then nothing will be left, except this guy who through no fault of his own will just be, like, *repellent* to me now, because he's just this other thing, with all of its own crap to deal with, just this extra burden on what I was carrying already? *Or.* If this is actually just unfixable now, if these feelings are just a *part* of me? Then is the right person someone who can just accept and *live* with them? And even if

I find someone who can, what if *I* can't? Like, what if that's not how I want to live? Like. What if there's a place in you that's only really touched when you get hurt. And nothing else can touch you in that place. But certain things *pretend* they can, and so your choices are to believe until you can't anymore, and really hurt someone, and I've really hurt some people, or to keep believing, to *make* yourself believe, and then get hurt yourself, again, in that same place? *Or* does the fact that *that's* what all this taught me mean that I've been doing absolutely *all* of it in some way *wrong*, that there's some other, better, way to do it, and that, every time, there is at least the chance I'll finally figure out what other way that is? *(beat)* You know?

ELLIOT. Yeah.

MOLLY. Really?

ELLIOT. Yes. Why is the cure always the beginning of the next disease?

MOLLY. Yeah.

ELLIOT. Let's keep an eye on that as well.

MOLLY. Yes, let's. *(beat)* So, wait, so what did we just decide?

ELLIOT. Um, I don't know, what do *you* think we just decided?

MOLLY. I asked you first.

ELLIOT. I know. And my response was to ask *you* what *you* think we –

MOLLY. Hey, you started this!

ELLIOT. What? No I didn't.

MOLLY. Yes you did!

ELLIOT. Well, okay, I mean, I invited you over to my *apartment*, but then you were the one who was like, "Yes, but I'm already in your apartment, right now, though, so – "

MOLLY. No, Elliot, you started this conversation by...! Never mind. *(beat)* "So how are you getting home?"

ELLIOT. Heh. Heh heh. Heh. *(pause)* Actually, now that you mention it, I *should* probably be...getting –

MOLLY. Oh, okay –

ELLIOT. No, just because... *(beat)* There's nothing more embarrassing than going public with something like this before you're sure, and so I don't want to get carried away. Before I do anything else I should really verify this thing. *(beat)* The algorithm.

MOLLY. Oh, right, no, of course.

ELLIOT. Yeah, as a wise woman once told me, that's why emergent properties are so mysterious: because, even when the result is right in front of you, you're nowhere if can't explain how it was reached.

MOLLY. You have to make sure the answers it's producing are actually correct.

ELLIOT. That's right. *(beat)* In a way, I'm *glad*. That I still have more *work* to do on it, you know? Because once I know I've really done it? This *thing* that I've been, like, striving towards for...? *Then*, it'll just be like...

MOLLY. Yeah. What happens now? *(pause)* So, yeah, I guess we should –

ELLIOT. Yeah, let's...

(**ELLIOT** *and* **MOLLY** *start to get dressed for real. This may involve just putting on the rest of their clothes, which are scattered around, or, for* **MOLLY**, *may involve getting new clothes entirely, this being her place, but regardless, they pick up their strewn clothing, and dress, in silence, for a moment. Then:)*

MOLLY. *(indicating the bathroom)* Do you need the...?

ELLIOT. No, it's all you.

MOLLY. Okay.

(**MOLLY** *goes into the bathroom.* **ELLIOT** *finishes dressing, looks around at the things in* **MOLLY**'s *room, really taking in the space. Maybe checks himself in a mirror. During this there is, perhaps, faintly, the sound of a computer working, some shift in light, and* **KATIE**

enters. She shares the space with **ELLIOT***, touching him
once maybe, then, moving around, performing some
banal tasks, like it's her apartment.* **MOLLY** *emerges from
the bathroom.* **CLARK** *follows her out, and now likewise
shares the space, moving around, doing boring stuff.
Perhaps* **MOLLY** *checks herself in a mirror as well, or just
starts to make the bed. Perhaps* **ELLIOT** *joins in, helps
her finish making the bed. Regardless, they ignore* **KATIE**
and **CLARK***, and focus on putting themselves, and the
room, back together. And is it, in fact, this focus on each
other that drives* **CLARK** *and* **KATIE** *from the room?
Maybe. In any case, by the end of this silent sequence,*
CLARK *and* **KATIE** *are gone.* **MOLLY** *settles in to work
and* **ELLIOT** *has his bag on. He looks at her. Then:)*

MOLLY. I'm just figuring out how to branch out a little,
cause there may be some problems with my...funding,
so –

ELLIOT. What if I worked here?

MOLLY. What?

ELLIOT. Well, I have my computer, so, what if I worked
here, on *my* stuff, while you work on yours. Like we'd
both be working, on different things, but in the same,
shared –

MOLLY. No, I gotcha, yeah –

ELLIOT. Unless you don't *want* me to, or –

MOLLY. No, no, I think I'd really like that.

ELLIOT. Well okay then.

MOLLY. Yeah. *(then, simply, quietly, still in the emotional mode
of the above)* See I wanted to do something called a
genetic knockout, where you make an organism that
has your protein *missing,* because seeing what happens
without it gives you clues to what it's for, and I wanted
to do it in creatures that are the most like us, but,
apparently, the result, in this case, would be too severe.
It kills the mice.

(...transition...)

8.

(the Molecular Biology Departmental office)

(MOLLY *is here with* **FRANKLIN.** *He is looking at a computer printout.)*

FRANKLIN. He said this wasn't accurate?

MOLLY. Yeah.

FRANKLIN. That's ridiculous.

MOLLY. Well –

FRANKLIN. You know what I think's going on?

MOLLY. What.

FRANKLIN. I think it's generational.

MOLLY. Oh –

FRANKLIN. I mean, whatever, I know Professor Davis is only six, seven years older than we are? But it makes a difference. To your comfort level with certain things, or what you're suspicious of, so when he hears these numbers came out of a computer you might as well be saying you waved a magic wand. He doesn't trust it.

MOLLY. Well, it's complicated.

FRANKLIN. Of course it's *complicated* but as someone whose responsibility is, in part, to remain up to date with advances in the field – ?

MOLLY. No, I –

FRANKLIN. And, yeah, he's your advisor, you're protective of him, I get it, all I'm saying? His reputation in the department?

MOLLY. Uh, what.

FRANKLIN. Just kind of hidebound, inflexible. *All* these guys, honestly.

MOLLY. Oh. *(beat)* Yeah he said that computational approaches were fashionable but unreliable.

FRANKLIN. Just like my ex-girlfriend. *(beat)* Sorry, other people's pain, nobody's interested. Point is, this *old* model? Of, oh, we're MB&B, over there's C.S., that's

Chemistry, that's Physics, in ten years? Mark my words, *all* those barriers will be *down*, they will look *laughable*, this whole reductionist approach will be obsolete and Science, *all* of Science, will move inexorably toward *integration*, toward rigorous methods of integration that *necessarily rely* on interdisciplinary cooperation, and if you were at a different University? Where this culture had already taken hold? And there *are* some? None of this would have been a problem. In fact it's what would have been *required* of you.

MOLLY. Well, thanks, Franklin, I appreciate it.

FRANKLIN. Please, I was *pissed*, I mean, this has implications for us *all*, potentially.

MOLLY. Well I'm glad to hear you say that because, actually, I was wondering...

FRANKLIN. What.

MOLLY. I was wondering if I could use your mice.

FRANKLIN. What?

MOLLY. Oh not to *take* them, to *breed* them, you've... Since I can't get *new* mice right now, and since you *have* mice to which you have already given various genetic ailments, *I'm* thinking what if I just produce offspring from *your* mice, do a targeted *insertion* of Protein M, and see what preexisting conditions your mice *already* have get *cured*.

FRANKLIN. Ah. The ever-popular gene knock-*in*.

MOLLY. Yeah, which may take several generations, some mutation, but will, eventually, plateau at the most likely interpretation of my protein's role.

FRANKLIN. Yeah. I mean, you'd also need to add, like, a reporter gene that turns the affected mice a different color – ?

MOLLY. Oh, yeah, I –

FRANKLIN. I like blue.

MOLLY. Me too! *(beat)* So, wait, is that a yes?

FRANKLIN. I don't know. How specific can you get with your predictions?

MOLLY. Aha. What if I told you that I also have a computer model of my protein's interaction network in which I have already run, virtually, the experiment I just described?

FRANKLIN. Why, are you...about to tell me that?

MOLLY. Yes.

FRANKLIN. Seriously?

MOLLY. Yeah.

FRANKLIN. Did you...make that *yourself*, or – ?

MOLLY. Oh, no no, I –

FRANKLIN. See!? This is what I'm *talking* about! Cooperation! You went outside the department, right?

MOLLY. Yeah to this, uh...this other grad student, just this...grad student in C.S.

(**MOLLY** *makes note of her own evasiveness as* **FRANKLIN** *goes on, heedlessly.*)

FRANKLIN. That is so fantastic. I have been trying to convince MB&B to look into computer modeling for, well, since I got here, so for longer than I care to... But that is *great*. I mean, *I* totally need one of those. Or, do you think it's adaptable, or, could I just *look* at it?

MOLLY. Yeah of course.

FRANKLIN. *Great*. Could, are you free right now, or – ?

MOLLY. We...Franklin, we have to teach in like five minutes.

FRANKLIN. Oh that's right. Fucking undergrads.

MOLLY. But, I mean, *after* class –

FRANKLIN. No, that's no good for me, um...Are you free tonight?

MOLLY. Oh, um... I mean, yeah, but –

FRANKLIN. Okay. Great. *(beat)* Or, I mean, I'm not asking you *out* or anything, I...Not that I'm not interested, I mean, you're *very*...Or, but, not that I'm assuming *you'd* be interested, just, it's more, as I just *intimated*, I am quite *recently*, uhhh...So I would probably not be good for *anyone* or *anything* right now except for, you know, something that's just really really... *(beat)* You did not need to know any of those things.

MOLLY. No, it's fine, I... *(beat)* Just let me make a quick...

(MOLLY takes out her phone and dials. Lights up on ELLIOT's office. A cell phone rings on the desk. NELL is here, sitting near, but not at, the desk. She looks over at the phone. Looks around. Should she answer it? She leans over towards the phone to see who's calling. MOLLY hangs up and the phone goes silent. NELL sits back. MOLLY turns to FRANKLIN who has been waiting patiently.)

I actually always thought you hated me.

FRANKLIN. What? Why? What? No. Why would you...? No. Why?

MOLLY. Oh, just because, I'm always...late, and, like –

FRANKLIN. Oh, that's, no, hey, teaching *sucks*, I get it. No, no, I think...I think we're probably very similar, you and me.

(MOLLY and FRANKLIN exit together, as ELLIOT enters his office, to find NELL.)

ELLIOT. Hey, sorry, I –

NELL. Your phone rang.

ELLIOT. What?

NELL. You missed a call. Your –

ELLIOT. *(going to check his phone)* Oh, okay. Umm...

NELL. Am I in trouble?

ELLIOT. What?

NELL. Well, I know that my heuristics problem set was late, and that my brute force problem set was *very* late, in that I've not yet turned it in? But I've been going through something of a personal crisis, which, okay, I know –

ELLIOT. Nell.

NELL. I know is not a legitimate excuse, like, scholastically, but as a, like, mitigating circumstance – ?

ELLIOT. *(overlapping)* Nell. Nell.

NELL. What.

ELLIOT. Relax. I just need your help with something.

NELL. Oh.

ELLIOT. Yeah. Here.

(**ELLIOT** *tosses* **NELL** *a very large computer printout.*)

NELL. Ah! What's this?

(beat)

ELLIOT. Do you know what a two-hybrid screen is?

NELL. Um, no, look, like I said, I haven't really been so good lately about –

ELLIOT. It's, no, we didn't cover it in class. This is molecular biology.

NELL. Oh.

ELLIOT. Yeah, okay, here's what's happening: I have designed an algorithm that produces answers to NP-Complete problems inside polynomial time *but* the only way to know for *sure* that an answer it's producing is actually correct would be to *already have* the answer in hand to compare that answer *to* which is something of a vicious cycle as you can I am sure see so what I actually *need* is: a problem that's NP-Complete when you try to tackle it all at *once* but which has *already been solved*, piecemeal, in some other way.

(beat)

NELL. You designed *what?*

ELLIOT. I have designed an algorithm –

NELL. Oh no I heard you. Is this *it?*

ELLIOT. Ah. No. *That* is the most complete map, to date, of the protein interaction network, or, um, interactome, of the common, or "house", mouse.

NELL. Okay.

ELLIOT. Yes. Through painstaking research the world over molecular biologists have successfully identified many, though not near all, of the protein-protein interactions that take place inside the various cells and matrices of our friend the mouse, which, given how many proteins that is, represents an exponentially large number of potential pairings. A two-hybrid screen is a wet experiment which, by recreating the binding or the failure to bind of these proteins, in yeast cultures, like so...? *(he pulls* **MOLLY***'s original Petri dish out of his back pocket)* Can be used either to confirm or to explode predictions regarding the network, with me so far?

NELL. Yeast cultures, seriously?

ELLIOT. *(already opening up the simulation on his computer)* I have arranged my algorithm to mimic a massive yeast two-hybrid screen, like that Petri dish but much much larger, capable of checking every known mouse protein against every other known mouse protein and telling us what interacts, and, since we *have* the *answers,* we will know whether our simulation gets it right. So. I am going to run this and monitor its progress. *You* are going to check the results against the pre-existing data. Ready?

NELL. Are we...doing this right now?

ELLIOT. Do you have time? This could take a while.

NELL. I, yeah, I have... Sure.

    *(***ELLIOT*** glances at his phone again.)*

ELLIOT. Great. Um, actually, just let me make a quick –

NELL. Oh, yeah, of course.

    *(***NELL*** retreats to a slight distance. ***ELLIOT*** opens his phone. Then changes his mind, puts the phone away, and starts to type an email on his laptop. Then, ***NELL***, having let everything sink in:)*

NELL. Uhhh... Why me?

ELLIOT. Oh, umm... *(He sends his email with a "send" noise.)* Well, this is not the kind of thing I want to bring up with my professors and turn out to be wrong about. And as for my direct peers, if I tell them I have a solution to a major problem they'd certainly be eager to poke holes in it, but maybe not in the most unbiased, scientific way, so –

NELL. What about your girlfriend?

ELLIOT. What?

NELL. That chick Lauren? In C.S.? She was my T.A. *last* semester and she talked about you a lot. A *lot*, she –

ELLIOT. Yeah, umm…that is not an option anymore.

NELL. Oh. Okay.

ELLIOT. Yeah. Which, um, which leaves undergraduates.

NELL. I see. So you *settled*, in other words.

ELLIOT. I, heh, no I, um… *(beat)* I think that you're brave. *(beat)* Or, I mean, it is *traditional* to be assisted in one's work by one's students, and you seem, more than your classmates, to have an essential quality that will prevent you from falling into certain, um… *(beat)* I chose you specifically, okay?

(beat)

NELL. Okay.

ELLIOT. Okay. Here goes.

(ELLIOT turns back to his computer clicks his mouse. At this, a line of computer code prints, unobtrusively, across an upper corner of a back wall of the space, say. Perhaps we don't even notice it at first. But it says:)

(Generating Init.Pop…)

(Also, at the same time, MOLLY and FRANKLIN return, now in yet another space: MOLLY's apartment. MOLLY heads straight for her computer.)

FRANKLIN. I like your place.

MOLLY. Thanks. Me too. I, here, I have it on my…And, actually, you can open up the underlying code, to see what it's doing while it…

(MOLLY has opened up the simulation on her laptop and clicks to run it and to open up the code. Thus, again, elsewhere:)

(Generating Init.Pop...)

ELLIOT. This first part is random but soon it will start matching proteins in a systematic way, and then we can...

MOLLY. *(overlapping on "start")* Right now it's of course set to simulate the ECM of mouse cartilage but it can probably mimic anything, so...

(During this, first one line of code, and then the other, are replaced:)

(Init.Pop Full)

(Meanwhile, NELL looks at ELLIOT and FRANKLIN puts a hand on MOLLY's back.)

NELL. Hey.

MOLLY. What.

(NELL kisses ELLIOT. FRANKLIN kisses MOLLY. MOLLY and ELLIOT kiss them back. Then MOLLY and ELLIOT both break away. A moment. Then an email arrives on MOLLY's computer with an "arrival" noise.)

FRANKLIN. *(pointing)* Email.

(And, with that, lines of code start to run down the walls, onto the floors, looking something like this:)

```
if (E > F)
then                        if (M > N)
{select.crossover(E)}       then
else                        {select.crossover(M)}
{select.crossover(F)}       else
end if                      {select.crossover(N)}
                            end if

if (F > G)
then                        if (N > O)
{select.crossover(F)}       then
```

```
else                              {select.crossover(N)}
{select.crossover(G)              else
end if                            {select.crossover(O)}
                                  end if

if (G > H)
then                              if (O > P)
{select.crossover(G)}             then
else                              {select.crossover(O)}
{select.crossover(H)}             else
end if                            {select.crossover(P)}
                                  end if

if (H > I)
then                              if (P > Q)
{select.crossover(H)}             then
if (I > J)                        {select.crossover(P)}
then
{select.crossover(I)}             if (Q > R)
                                  then
                                  {select.crossover(Q)}

if (J > K)
                                  if (R > S)

if (K > L)
                                  if (S > T)

if (L > M)
                                  if (T > U)
```

(...and so on, through the alphabet, faster and faster. Along with this, a sound we now recognize, of a hard drive straining and trying to cool itself, begins, and swells, this time not localized to a particular computer on the set, but rather coming from everywhere. A transition begins: **FRANKLIN** *and* **NELL** *exit, leaving* **ELLIOT** *and* **MOLLY** *alone. The code fills the space more and more and the sound builds. Then* **ELLIOT** *and* **MOLLY** *themselves begin to exit, trying to continue the transition, but then, suddenly, as the technical spectacle around them reaches its peak...the sound cuts out, the code vanishes, and the lights freeze in a strange, mostly dark, intermediate*

cue. **ELLIOT** *and* **MOLLY**, *still on stage, are caught awkwardly in mid-exit. Perhaps they glance at one another. Then they scurry off.* **MOLLY** *quietly mutters, "Not again." Then, for a few moments, the stage is empty, in this odd cue, the only sound the faint, gentle tick of a computer, somewhere, still working. Then from backstage, someone calls: "Can we get some more light?" The work lights come on. Then, after another moment, the actors playing* **FRANKLIN** *and* **NELL** *emerge. There is a loose, improvisatory energy to what follows.)*

FRANKLIN. *(to the audience)* Hey, sorry about that –

NELL. *(overlapping)* Yeah, sorry.

FRANKLIN. This, uhhhhh…This has been happening? On occasion? When –

NELL. Yeah, at this point in the show –

FRANKLIN. Yeah, presumably because of the intensity of the whole technical sequence just there, which –

NELL. Yeah apparently what can happen here is that the whole board just…freezes?

FRANKLIN. No. Sort of. Not really.

NELL. Or, okay, I guess that's not technically precisely exactly what's happening? But the point is, what we've learned is that rather than resetting? That the best thing to do is to wait for it to…unfreeze.

FRANKLIN. And so what has been, um, *decided* is that, if this happens, rather than there being some impersonal announcement from the stage manager, while all of us just disappear, and let you sit here in the dark wondering what the hell is happening, that we, *(Here he says the actual name of the actor playing* **NELL**.*)* and I –

NELL. Hello.

FRANKLIN. – since we do not appear for the remainder of the play –

NELL. *(Here she says the actual name of the actor playing* **FRANKLIN**.*)* –

FRANKLIN. That we will come out, and tell you what is actually going on. On the theory that it's better...if you know something's actually...happening...

(beat)

NELL. This should be over very soon.

FRANKLIN. Yes.

NELL. It never takes very long.

FRANKLIN. And, but, you know what? If it turns out we can't fix it, that's okay, too, because, regardless, our stalwart fellow cast members, *(here she says the actual name of the actor playing* **MOLLY***)* and *(here she says the actual name of the actor playing* **ELLIOT***)*, will come back out, and complete the play for you in any case. Which, in my experience, is all that this stuff really needs, just... people... *(pause)* In a room... *(pause)* And...time... *(beat)* In fact, let's just try that for a second, while we have a chance...to, humor me, and just, be here, with us, silently, while we wait, just breathing, for a moment, starting...now...

(Then, **FRANKLIN** *and* **NELL** *just stand there, looking out at the audience. Being with them. Silence. Stillness. This is at first probably awkward. Then, perhaps, truly connected. Until finally the silence feels full. Throbbing. Mystical. At which point, perhaps* **FRANKLIN** *glances towards the back of the house, to the booth...the transition picks up from where it left off,* **FRANKLIN** *and* **NELL** *exit...and we land at last in...)*

9.

(the public computer cluster)

*(**MOLLY** enters, puts her jacket over the back of a chair, and sits at one of the computers. She types for a while. Then **ELLIOT** enters. A moment. She turns and sees him.)*

ELLIOT. Hey.

MOLLY. Hey. *(then, pretending she was just leaving, putting on her jacket:)* I was actually just…

ELLIOT. Oh, okay.

MOLLY. Yeah, so –

ELLIOT. Or, could I maybe talk to you for a second?

MOLLY. Oh, uhhh… *(beat)* Yeah, okay.

ELLIOT. Okay. *(pause)* How've you been?

MOLLY. Good. You?

ELLIOT. Good, yeah, good. Good. *(pause)* I, um, I *have* something for you.

MOLLY. What?

ELLIOT. Yeah, it's… I got it for you back when we were… But I haven't seen you in a while, so I've been carrying around in my bag for weeks like an idiot, I… Here…

*(**ELLIOT** has been rummaging in his bag and now pulls out a bottle of whiskey.)*

MOLLY. Is that whiskey?

ELLIOT. Yeah, it's…

MOLLY. You know, I'm not, like, a *lush* or anything.

ELLIOT. No, I know, I just…I don't know for sure anything else you like? Except for *sex*, and I already…got you that, like, a bunch of times, so –

MOLLY. *(taking the bottle)* Thank you.

ELLIOT. You're welcome. Also for the whiskey.

MOLLY. Uh-huh.

(beat)

ELLIOT. So —

MOLLY. Listen, Elliot, I get it.

ELLIOT. What do you get.

MOLLY. What it's like when…it's amazing. And I'm sure it's going to change your life, and, so, you don't have to explain, I —

ELLIOT. It doesn't work.

MOLLY. What?

ELLIOT. The algorithm. It doesn't work. Or, I mean, it *works*, it applies…biological rules to mathematical propositions and produces *answers* but the *problem* is: actual living things, in the, like, real world? Are affected by it. By the world. So no matter how many levels of complexity you add to the simulation all you're getting are more and more refined answers generated from the inside, out, you're missing the… other half, the, everything that runs from outside, in, so you don't just need an exponentially increasing number of membranes in the simulation itself, you would need an exponentially increasing number of *other independent* simulations sending answers to one another, to be taken in, again, and then sent back out, and so on, and, without that, the versions of these problems that it's solving are not, in fact, analogous to one another, at all, and so cannot be considered NP-Complete, and so it is, in the end, useless, except as applied, one at a time, to every single hyper-specific case.

MOLLY. You made a derivation error.

ELLIOT. That is what it's called.

MOLLY. When did you figure that out?

ELLIOT. It was, um…pointed out to me?

MOLLY. When though.

ELLIOT. Um, recently.

MOLLY. Ah.

ELLIOT. What.

MOLLY. Let's just say your sudden desire to talk to me is starting to make sense.

ELLIOT. Oh come on.

MOLLY. What, I haven't heard from you in weeks, so –

ELLIOT. I, okay, may I point out that *I* also haven't heard from *you* in weeks?

MOLLY. Well right but that's because I wasn't hearing from you.

ELLIOT. Except I'm pretty sure the last communiqué came from me.

MOLLY. I, okay, I suppose that *technically* that's true? But it was I think you'll admit relatively spare and remote and came only after I reached out to you a couple of times and so I got the message and backed off a little myself and then I didn't hear from you again.

ELLIOT. I wasn't hearing from you!

MOLLY. What did I *just explain?*

ELLIOT. Well…! *(beat)* I'm here now.

MOLLY. Yeah. Who's Nell?

ELLIOT. What?

MOLLY. No, just, who's this girl "Nell", I'm – ?

ELLIOT. I, she's…! Why, who's "Franklin"?

MOLLY. Oh so we're going to do *this* now.

ELLIOT. *What?* You *started* it!

MOLLY. No. *You* did.

ELLIOT. I did not!

MOLLY. Yes! You did! By claiming to be "here" now!

ELLIOT. But…I am!

MOLLY. If you say so, Elliot, but it doesn't really matter cause I'm leaving.

ELLIOT. Okay. Where are you going? I'll come with you.

MOLLY. No. No, I'm… *(beat)* I'm leaving *town*.

ELLIOT. What? When?

MOLLY. At the end of the semester, I'm…transferring.

ELLIOT. Transferring.

MOLLY. Yeah.

ELLIOT. As in: "to a different graduate school" transferring?

MOLLY. Uh, yeah.

ELLIOT. Where?

MOLLY. I don't know. I mean, not *yet*, first I'm…just going *home*, to…regroup, see Mom, and then…yeah, onto the next place. I heard about some programs where there's more of a culture of like, cooperative…? So I applied to a bunch of those and I should know exactly where I'll land by Spring.

ELLIOT. When were you going to tell *me?*

MOLLY. What do you mean?

ELLIOT. Well, so, if I hadn't *happened* into this room *today* I'd just have *heard* that you were *gone?*

MOLLY. Hey, if *I* hadn't "happened into this room" that other day you'd never have had to know that I was even here in the *first* place.

ELLIOT. I…! *What?* That's…! *So?*

MOLLY. Well…!

ELLIOT. I just… *(beat)* I mean, is this because of *funding*, or – ?

MOLLY. Oh, no, I sort of…worked that out? But I still just… I don't know. I guess it just felt like…time.

ELLIOT. Oh. So…that's you then.

MOLLY. Yeah. That's me.

(Long pause. Perhaps we think the play might be ending. But then:)

ELLIOT. Want to hear a joke? *(beat)* Guy walking down the street at night sees a scientist under a streetlamp looking for something in the gutter. Says, "Hey, is there a problem?" Scientist says, "Yes, actually, I dropped my car keys, and I can't seem to find them." Guy says, "I'll help you look." But after a while of searching and searching and not finding anything the guy looks up and says, "Are you sure that this is where you dropped your keys?" Scientist says, "No, actually, I dropped them over there." And he points to a dark alley about halfway down the block. And the guy says, "Then what the hell are we looking *here* for then?" And the Scientist says, "This is where the light is." *(pause)* You know, I've been…coming to this computer cluster, a lot, lately, just at random, different times of day, just…even though it's not remotely convenient for me, or on my way anywhere, but just because I've been I guess…*hoping*…and I know that I probably could have *written* to you, or…called, I guess, but for some reason I felt like I was supposed to just… *(beat)* Molly, I really like you?

MOLLY. That's fantastic, Elliot.

ELLIOT. No, like, really a lot, and I'm attracted to you, and you're really smart, and we're interested in a lot of the same things, and I look forward to seeing you, and I think about you when you're not around, and so if I seem spare, or remote, well, then, I'm sorry that I seem that way, but I *promise* it has nothing to with not wanting to be close to you, or…wanting to be with *other* people, or, okay, I mean, it does, of course it does, a *little*, I mean, sure, I want to sleep with every attractive woman I meet, or pass on the street, or am told about second hand, I mean, you people don't know what it's like, you *think* you do, and maybe you *kind of* do, in your way, but you don't, not really, you do not… Not that I actually want to go out and actually *sleep* with lots of people, that's an awful lot of *work*, and it usually turns out to be more trouble than it's *worth*, and, I'm getting off topic? What it *is* is: the fear that actually knowing everything about each other will eliminate the wanting. And so maybe what I was hoping was that, this time, if I could hold something just close enough to keep it from disappearing, but just far away enough to maintain how I *felt* about it, which was good, by the way, this felt really really good, then maybe I could draw this first part out a little, because, I don't know about you? But I don't have any compelling evidence that something better after this? Even exists. That it ever gets any better than still wanting to be with you, and still knowing that I can, or...*could*, because this obviously doesn't work either, does it, so... Maybe, what's req... *(beat)* I'm so tired. Of going back and forth. Between failing at this and wondering why I failed. *(beat)* I want us to know everything about each other. I want us to know so much it turns out we know less and less every day. *(beat)* Sorry. Too much? Too soon?

MOLLY. No. *(beat)* You know, it's not...*totally* useless.

ELLIOT. What?

MOLLY. The algorithm.

ELLIOT. Oh.

MOLLY. I mean, *I* used it. Just, for what it was originally intended: to make a prediction about the function of an unknown protein, and then test it, live. Turns out it does good things for mice with damage in a particular area, though, in fact, a couple other proteins do more or less the same thing, and so it could be it's a redundancy, or possibly even something we found *already* and *mistook* for something new, but until proven otherwise we're treating it as a unique molecule, and have even, provisionally at least, named it. For its particular usefulness in aiding cell migration.

ELLIOT. Yeah? What'd you call it?

MOLLY. Travelin. *(beat)* Anyway, now I have a little more information to go back and do my next screen.

ELLIOT. Bait and Prey. *(beat)* Are you gonna say anything about what I just said?

MOLLY. What do you want me to say, Elliot? I... *(beat)* I mean, thank you. For saying all of that. But this is still probably not a very good time for me to...For either of us, really, for something like this...For, just, you know *what?* This is just a terrible time in all our lives. And a terrible *terrible* generation to be a part of. To know *just enough* to know that this stuff never works but *not* enough to know what the fuck we're supposed to *do* about it. *(beat)* I will never be a clean slate. I will never be a clean slate. Again. So…

*(A moment. **MOLLY** turns to walk away.)*

ELLIOT. Whoa, where are you going?

MOLLY. I just have to go.

ELLIOT. Right now? Really?

MOLLY. Yes. Or, no, I just, I… *(beat; then, quietly)* I just really really have to pee.

ELLIOT. Oh. *(then, proudly)* Still got it

MOLLY. Shut *up*, it's not *you*, it… That was an extremely long speech. And I appreciate it. And I have to go.

*(**MOLLY** turns to go again.)*

ELLIOT. Can I come with you?

MOLLY. What?

ELLIOT. Can I come with you.

MOLLY. To…pee?

ELLIOT. No, when you go, when you –

MOLLY. You want to come *with* me?

ELLIOT. Yeah. *(beat)* Why, how are you getting there, did you already by a plane ticket, or are you driving or – ?

MOLLY. I, that's not, who cares! Elliot!

ELLIOT. What.

MOLLY. You can't come *with* me, that's *insane!*

ELLIOT. Why?

MOLLY. Because…! It's…! *(beat)* I mean what if I said *yes?*

ELLIOT. What?

MOLLY. What if I said, yeah, sure, pack your things, come with me, let's just see where this goes. What then?

ELLIOT. Well… *(beat)* I mean is that what you're saying?

MOLLY. What if it is?

ELLIOT. Is it, though?

MOLLY. What if it is?

ELLIOT. Yeah but is it?

MOLLY. *What if it is?*

ELLIOT. I don't know! I just…! *(beat)* I mean now I'm a little nauseous.

MOLLY. Maybe you're pregnant.

ELLIOT. You're right, that joke's not funny.

(A long silence. There is just the ambient sound of all the computers. Then, at last **MOLLY** *offers her hand. For a handshake. A moment.* **ELLIOT** *shakes* **MOLLY***'s hand. The handshake complete,* **MOLLY** *tries to pull her hand away. But she can't. Because* **ELLIOT** *is gently holding on. The handshake thus morphs into them holding hands.)*

ELLIOT. So…

MOLLY. So…?

ELLIOT. How are you getting home?

(Lights fade…first to blue…then to black…)

END OF PLAY